UNBOXING GOD

RECLAIMING FAITH IN A POST-CHURCH CULTURE

TAMARA J. BUCHAN

Tamara J Buchan
Reclaim Initiative
Morrison, CO 80465
www.ReclaimInitiative.com

Cover and Interior Design: Brenda Emmert, brenda.emmert11@gmail.com
Editor: Charleeda Sprinkle, charleeda@gmail.com

If Scriptures are quoted but not italicized, they have been
paraphrased by the author.

Unboxing God/ Tamara J. Buchan. -- 1st ed.
ISBN-13: 978-0-578-42303-6

Printed in the United States of America

RECLAIM
INITIATIVE

DEDICATION

I dedicate this book to all those who sense God is bigger than the box you currently know Him within and who are willing to let Him enlarge or dismantle your box.

- To those who have walked faithfully with God all their lives doing the right things but are weary and wondering how they can live differently

- To those who have stopped going to the organized church out of frustration, despair, or a nagging sense that something isn't quite right

- To those who used to be satisfied with status quo in their faith but are hungrily searching out the deeper things of God's Kingdom

- To those who are actively pursuing the King and His Kingdom

I've been there…in all these places. All I can say is that the *pursuit is worth it*. May the Lord meet you as you journey through this book, and may He give you all that you need to take the next step towards Him, and the next…until your heart is fully saturated by His unboxed love.

FOREWORD

Are you an explorer? Do you enjoy taking back trails when you hike? Do you like deep sea diving? How about skydiving or bungee jumping? Or perhaps you're the scientific type who enjoys staring endlessly into a microscope watching microbes move around or maybe you want to be one of the first people to experience space flight or cure cancer.

I have discovered that there are two kinds of explorers. There are those who return from their exploits saying; "Wow, you should've seen what I saw" and then there are those like my friend, Tamara Buchan, who return with a *map* guiding others to the place of her discovery.

In the 15th Century, a wealthy Venetian Senator asked a cartographer to create a map of Venice. He returned with a map of Italy on which Venice appeared as a small dot. The Senator ordered the mapmaker to redo the map and make Venice larger. Maps are always subjective and limited in scope.

Unboxing God: Reclaiming Faith in a Post-Church Culture is a map of Tamara's journey in following Jesus into and out of the Church. Sometimes her map shows a Church that appears large and influential but at other times it's small and distant. She reminds us of the lost message of the centrality of the Kingdom of God and wonders out loud about why the Church and seekers have to be at odds with each other. She goes out "into the field" and explores how the other half lives on Sunday mornings while many of us are in our churches singing and listening to professional Christians remind us why we need to keep coming back. She asks importantly how the Church became more focused around right beliefs than around experiences with God.

As a self designated, spiritual anthropologist, I have been exploring religious spirituality for fifty years with a specialty in evangelicalism. Like Tamara, I have tried to create maps for people who are not natural spiritual explorers but are willing to travel if you can give them a map that provides them enough guidance to travel to new places in their spiritual lives.

I have almost no curiosity about the natural world, such as mountains and lakes, but if someone I admired or loved invited me on a hike and I knew they had a map, I could be tempted to travel with them. Maybe you aren't a natural spiritual explorer like Tamara. Maybe you can't imagine God telling you to "stop going to church" or like the Apostle Peter, to eat with the Gentiles. Not to worry. In *Unboxing God: Reclaiming Faith in a Post-Church Culture*, Tamara Buchan translates her explorations into a map you can use to reacquaint yourself with the people Jesus misses most – the people formerly known as lost simply by not going to church on Sunday, and instead, hanging out with them and practicing the lost art of *noticing* others.

It turns out that traveling into Tamara's world with Jesus doesn't require that you to physically travel but it does require you to suspend judgment, pay attention, and let go of preconceived notions you may have inherited from spending too much time in church and not enough in the world Jesus invited us to explore with him. In our day, the Church has earned a reputation that might be encapsulated in this slogan "Safety first, Jesus second". If that offends you, I highly recommend you spend time reflecting on and putting into practice some the ideas Tamara Buchan suggests in her wonderful new book, *Unboxing God: Reclaiming Faith in a Post-Church Culture*.

Jim Henderson D.Min
Author of *Jim and Casper Go to Church*
Executive Producer: Jim Henderson Presents

TABLE OF CONTENTS

INTRODUCTION

I sat in the church service devastated. My life and ministry had just been tossed up into the air and were dramatically falling down, piece by piece. As the pastor began to pray, something strange happened. I saw a big refrigerator box in my mind, and then I sensed God say, "You've had Me in a box, and I want to remove your boxes." Then, He took the box and began to rip the box apart, one side at a time. I didn't realize it then, but this was the start to a wild, wonderful, and often confusing and disorienting ride of my faith.

I am sharing my story because I wonder if perhaps you may recognize yourself within it. I was doing all the right things: reading my Bible, sharing Jesus with people, tithing to our church, and even giving my life to serve in ministry. But, deep down inside, I knew there was more to this walk of faith. I yearned to experience a life that resembled the believers after Pentecost with the miracles and community they experienced on a daily basis. But, then I'd look around and see my reality, people faithfully doing and saying the right things, but still rather stuck in their circumstances and challenges. I would realize, yet again, that I needed to wait for heaven to experience the communion Adam and Eve had in the Garden of Eden with God or the crazy miracles the new believers experienced after Jesus' ascension to heaven.

Interestingly, even though I tried to be content with my life of faith, God had other plans. It all started with the box experience, and now many years later, He is enjoying the journey of life together with me.

To set the stage for sharing my journey with you, it is important that we first acknowledge the season of history that we find ourselves within. We are in transition, much like the time of Pentecost in the beginning of Acts. I like to think about all that took place after that awe-inspiring day when the once fearful disciples left the upper room, went boldly into the Temple courtyard, where the very one who denied Jesus three times just 40 days earlier, stood up and preached the sermon of his life. Peter was so bold in his assertions that Jesus had been crucified, dead in the tomb for three days but then resurrected, and then ascended into heaven 50 days later, that 3,000 people responded with a "yes" to his invitation to follow Jesus and even to be baptized. It's not so farfetched to think that, just weeks before, many of them may have found themselves chanting, "Crucify Him! Crucify Him!"

After Pentecost, everything changed. The fearful disciples became bold apostles and began to call people to meet in homes after the Temple services. They saw big miracles take place; in fact, miracles became common place. They developed a community of support, of learning, and of sharing communion around the dinner table. The new Jesus followers were still Jewish, and they kept practicing the rituals of their Jewish faith, even as they walked out their new season of life.

It wasn't until Stephen was stoned to death that the new believers began to leave Jerusalem. This is where it gets interesting. They suddenly found themselves around the dinner table with those who previously had been declared unacceptable. Problems abounded because both Jews and Gentiles were being challenged to lay down the familiar and pick up the unfamiliar new practices of Jesus and His Kingdom ways.

Today, we find ourselves in a very similar period of shifting. The Church Season which I believe began after Constantine declared Christianity the legal religion in the fourth century, continued for close to 1,800 years. It was around the time of the emerging internet when everything began to change, launching a huge transition into the Kingdom Age. Transitions of this magnitude don't happen overnight, however, so the shift between the familiar Church Season and the rapidly advancing Kingdom Age may take up to 50 or 100 years to fully complete.

It's during these massive transitions that confusion and disorientation become commonplace. As I asked people how they defined the Kingdom, I found there was much confusion; many thinking that church and kingdom were the same. So, one day, I decided to write a concise, precise definition of the Kingdom. I looked up some of my heroes of faith to see how they defined the Kingdom. Interestingly, I didn't find many authors who attempted to define it, but I found three that were helpful.

Dallas Willard—professor of philosophy at the University of Southern California for 41 years and prolific author—defined it this way: "The range of God's effective will, where what God wants done is done. It is an everlasting metaphysical reality, the natural home of the soul: God and His reign 'from everlasting to everlasting.'"[1]

Mike Breen, founder of 3dm, describes the Kingdom in these words:

> The king of heaven has taken on flesh and chosen to walk among his wayward subjects, to reveal the future he has prepared for us, a future that we can taste now if only we will surrender to his Kingship. The King is a servant King who wants his people to be the greatest recipients of its benefits. In response to receiving all the blessings, the people of the King offer him their love, loyalty, glory and honor. The Kingdom of God is expressed in three key words: King, authority and power.[2]

Bill Johnson, senior pastor of Bethel Church in Redding, California, states, "The Kingdom of God is when everything in Heaven is instituted on the earth, so that God's government, teaching, worship, glory, and power are manifested here on earth, and the earth looks just like Heaven." [3]

I also looked up every Scripture I could find about how Jesus defined the Kingdom, and this is what I discovered. Jesus never *defined* the King-

---

1 http.//www.dwillard.org/resources/willardwords.asp
2 Breen, Mike. Covenant and the Kingdom, p. 228.
3 http.//www.fromhispresence.com/best-kingdom-of-god-illustration/

dom! He *pointed* to the Kingdom, and He pointed out *when* the Kingdom was present. I finally wrote this phrase at the end of my study: Jesus *described* the Kingdom, but He never once *defined* it. So, if it worked for Jesus, let's decide to let it work for us. We can have fun looking for all the clues, much like a treasure hunt, because each one of them will lead us right back to greater relationship with the King of the Kingdom.

> *Jesus described the Kingdom,*
> *but He never once defined it.*

I am personally very excited about the transition we find ourselves living because it is in the times of shifting that the Lord reveals Himself in a new way. Miracles increase. The Holy Spirit speaks through revelations, dreams, and visions, adding layers to how God communicates Himself to us. On the flip side, transitional periods are also opportunities for great divisions. Denominations, churches, and individuals decide if they think it is truly the Lord moving, or if it is something trying to counterfeit God.

Perhaps whole generations find themselves feeling misunderstood, misrepresented, and very disillusioned with the status quo. Others defend the status quo as "faithful Christianity," and the Body of Christ looks as if it's been all chopped up in the process.

I am telling my story in an attempt to speak to you wherever you find yourself. Perhaps you have diligently done the things you were trained to do to live as a "faithful Christian." Maybe you even went so far as to attend seminary and become one who is employed by the church or a Christian organization. Possibly, you were raised in a churched home, but as you began your life as a young adult, you find the traditional answers and practices no longer appeal to you or even bring you close to the God you long to know. Maybe you are so frustrated with all of it that you've given up and are exploring other pathways to know God.

Let me ask you some questions:

Do you feel different?

Do you feel restless and, possibly, even bored with
spiritual activities or church attendance that used to fulfill you?

Are you beginning to find excuses for why you aren't
available to do them?

Have you even stopped attending Bible study or church alto-
gether?

Are you feeling confused or guilty or both?

Even more, could you possibly be in ministry and spend more
time planning your escape route than writing your sermon?

If this describes you, be at peace. You are in the midst of making the
transition from the Church Season to the Kingdom Age. It doesn't always
come easily, *but the price is worth it.*

If you find yourself like me—knowing there's more, wanting more, but
not knowing how to find it—keep reading. God has brought you here because He wants to take your box and rip it to pieces, so that you can discover the life of freedom which comes from seeking Jesus and discovering
His Kingdom ways.

Let me warn you, however, if you start down the path of allowing God
to break down your box, there may be a moment when you realize that you
can't turn around and go back. The only way forward is to go…*forward.*
But, here's the good news. You aren't alone. The numbers of people who
are walking this path are growing every day, and one day, they will become
the majority.

Some of you may struggle to hear how I speak about my life with God. I actually have conversations with Him, often. Some people, even professors in seminary, told me that it wasn't okay to have conversations with God and especially not to talk about it, or even worse, write it down!

Here's the reality. In the opening chapters of the Bible, we find God and Adam and Eve engaged in a very real and recorded conversation. So, if it is okay with God to record our conversations, I hope it will be okay with you too. If it isn't, this book may not be a good fit for you.

Perhaps we might want to make this agreement: For this book, we will drop all our "religious" preconceived ideas. Let's ask God to give us a fresh look at an important part of life—our relationship with the One who created us, life with a loving Dad who is busy working behind the scenes to bring about our best, and One who sets a place for us at His great big dinner table. *Let's give God permission to unbox Himself with us.*

Jesus came to earth to give us a picture of His Dad, and He spent a lot of time journeying with His friends from one place to another. Take a moment now to envision yourself on a journey with Jesus, as His friend, and give Him permission to take you where He is *already* going.

I can say with confidence that if you seek to read this as an intellectual exercise or an academic pursuit, you will most likely miss the point. We already know way too much information. Our brains are stuffed full to the point of bursting. I think many of us are crying out for an "experience with God," one that will radically change the way we think, worship, and live our day-to-day lives.

One last word of encouragement: The end matter at the close of each chapter is created to help you bridge the gaps that currently keep you stuck at one side of the canyon unable to cross over. Don't skip over them. Consider that they are the conversations you and Jesus are experiencing as you journey down the road together! He really does care about you and how you think.

Now, let's get started!

CHAPTER 1

WHO KICKED ME OUT OF CHURCH? GOD-REALLY!

Whew! I was sitting in the church service in anticipation of our celebration luncheon for the Aids Experience Initiative our church had just completed. It was no small undertaking. I led the process of raising over $200,000 from our community and filling 7,500 Aids Caregiver Kits to send in shipping containers to Zambia and South Sudan. It felt good to know that after the luncheon, the Aids Experience would become a happy memory, but the massive effort it took to carry it off was now over.

Suddenly, I sensed God speak, "You don't have any more responsibilities here this month, so I don't want to see you here." I was stunned and more than a little confused. I replied, "But, God, it's Advent. Do You remember I wrote an advent book, *Seeking the Christmas Lamb: A Family Advent Handbook?*" He replied again, "I don't want to see you here."

In my mind, a gauntlet with jagged teeth came down and split something apart. Two hands then took the two sides and pushed them far apart from one another. I heard it again, "I don't want to see you here again. In fact, after you complete the Missio Lux Moments in January and February, unless you are invited to preach or teach, I don't want to see you *inside church buildings at all.*" (Missio Lux was the new church plant that I was called by my church to lead. It means "mission of light" in Latin.)

Huh? I was reeling from that conversation. I had spent my entire vocational career serving the church in a variety of different capacities. I received my call to ministry when I was a children's director at a large suburban church. When I graduated from seminary, I started an equipping ministry called The Journey Project, where we matched people's missional passions to existing organizations and built communities with those who served them.

> *Suddenly, I sensed God speak, "You don't have any more responsibilities here this month, so I don't want to see you here."*

Eighteen months into The Journey Project, my husband ended up getting a new job in Seattle. Our move resulted in a call to this medium-sized church in my denomination I was now serving in as the associate pastor to adults. I spent five years developing spiritual formation, healing and care ministries, as well as local missional opportunities to help equip disciples who were emotionally and spiritually healed and ready to give their lives to something bigger. It was in this context that God decided to do something bigger *in me*!

It started a little over a year before God's shocking directive to leave the church building. He was preparing me for that "shocker," but I didn't know it. Over a nine-month period, God had shown me in several supernatural experiences a structure for how a church could be organized that looked vastly different from the current church structure. Those revelatory experiences caused a restlessness in me that got harder and harder to ignore.

One October day during prayer, where I asked the Lord if He had any plans for me to fulfill that day, He gave me a strange directive. I was to go to my senior leader and tell him that I was interested in church planting. I thought that was strange because I hadn't been thinking about church planting at all, but I committed to do it in response to how the Lord directed me.

When we met for our weekly meeting that day, I took a deep breath and said, "I am thinking about church planting." He turned rather green and said, "You know you would need to gather 150 in a year, don't you?" The conversation went downhill from there as he was less than encouraging (to put it mildly), but the strangest thing happened when I left his office. I experienced the tangible presence of the Holy Spirit move through my body, and I sensed the Lord whisper, "Thank you."

Shortly after that, I went by myself to Willow Creek for an Innovative Church Conference. On the second day, as the speaker began to talk, I realized, "Oh, I am in so much trouble!" The Holy Spirit was dealing with me about the structure He'd already been showing me. I didn't need anyone else to give me ideas. He wanted me to trust in the structure *He* had shown me.

By lunchtime, I was a complete mess. I ran to my car weeping intensely. I heard the Lord say, "You don't believe I am going to do this [plant a church through you], do you?"

I said angrily, "NO, I certainly do not!" I saw myself out on the street without followers, without a call, without finances.

He gently said, "Watch and see what I do."

I wrote it all down, but when I returned home, life got busy and stressful, and I quickly forgot about my Willow wrestling match in the parking lot. That Christmas (still a year before God's "big surprise") came and went, but shortly after, the inner restlessness increased to a point where I often felt like I would explode. I went back and forth, telling myself that I was blessed to have such a great call where I had freedom to lead, had great team partners, and saw people's lives being transformed.

Why wasn't it enough?

We began to work on church budget in January. As I sat in the meetings, I heard several times, "By the time we pay the mortgage, the salaries, and the utilities, *we only have 10% left to fund the ministries.*" The last time I heard it, the structure that the Lord had creatively unveiled to me came back to my mind, and I remembered how He had shown me it should be flipped: Just 25% should go to pay for infrastructure, and 75% should be available for the work of the ministry.

A couple of weeks later, I got a call from our church chairman. She wanted me to come to a leadership team meeting; they had something important to speak to me about. I was curious and a bit anxious but was completely blown away when we met. It seems, unbeknown to me, both the senior pastor and the leadership team felt called to plant a church, and God had clearly shown them that I was the one to plant it. When the meeting was over and I was leaving the church building, it felt like God was jumping up and down in celebration saying, "Look what I did!"

In June, when the leadership team and I met to fully commit to the reality of planting a church, I heard them say, "Tamara, we know you. We know God speaks to you, and we trust you with the vision of what this church should be." When I heard that statement and felt their love and approval, I sensed God saying, "I've parted the waters. Now, go walk through them."

REFLECT

- What stood out to you the most in this chapter?
- What do you think God might be saying to you through it?

DO SOMETHING

- Contact someone you know who left the organized church and have a conversation with them about it. Listen to their story and seek to understand.

CHAPTER 2

THE STRUGGLE: CHURCH IS IN MY PORES

Can you imagine what the month of December held after God gave me the boot? I felt like Abraham must have felt when he told Sarah that God wanted them to move. When I told my husband and our children, their confusion was tangible. It went pretty much like this:

"Well, where are we going?"

"Uh, I am not sure. He just said I can't come back to the service this month."

"What are we going to do on Christmas Eve?"

"Um…I am not sure. What would you like to do?"

Sunday mornings, which used to be my favorite time of the week, became something I dreaded with everything within me. It was agony to wake up and wonder what to do. Read the Sunday paper? I hadn't done that in years, as I was usually running out of the door while still putting on my shoes. Watch the football game? Talk with my neighbors? Go to the grocery store?

Here's what I realized. *A lot of life happens while we go to church on Sunday mornings.* Neighbors spend time chatting on their sidewalks. Lots of people go to the grocery store. Coffee shops are packed with families and groups, everyone happily chatting while drinking their designer coffees. Parks are full of teams playing sports, while parents watch excitedly from the sidelines. I began to wonder what I'd been missing all those years spent inside the church building.

> *Sunday mornings, which used to be my favorite time of the week, became something I dreaded with everything within me.*

So, after a couple of miserable Sunday mornings, when I wandered aimlessly around the house, I decided to give it a try and join the mass of people that were experiencing life—*outside the church building*.

I chatted with my neighbors. They were talking about the latest film they had just seen, and I was able to offer a valuable perspective to their conversation. They began to open up about their latest struggles with their children, and I ended up offering to pray for them. As we stood there huddled close together, we experienced the presence of God. I felt their tangible sense of relief that someone was giving them much needed support. I suddenly had a fleeting thought: *Could this be why God kicked me out of church?* Perhaps I was to bring the church to them.

> *A lot of life happens while we go to church on Sunday mornings.*

Christmas Eve was painful. I must say it made my whole body hurt. I grew up in the church and can still remember being very young but absorbing the sense of belonging as we lit our candles in the dark while singing "Silent Night." I still cherish singing the traditional Christmas carols. That Christmas, the closest I got was singing by myself to my Christmas music. My heart felt broken.

Our family talked it over and decided that we should go somewhere that celebrated light, so we went to the Botanical Gardens. I walked forlornly through it, barely enjoying the light show because all I could feel was disoriented. *What in the world was God thinking?* Did I hear Him right? How could He want me, His faithful servant, outside the church? Didn't He see all the good I was doing?

It took a couple of years to recognize what the two hands were pushing apart that day when God kicked me out of church. It was when I was reading through a Bible I hadn't used for a while that I saw a date posted next to Luke 9:1-2. I suddenly realized it was the Saturday of the fateful weekend when I got the boot.

> *I suddenly had a fleeting thought: Could this be why God kicked me out of church? Perhaps I was to bring the church to them.*

Then I remembered what I had sensed God say to me regarding Luke 9:1-2, "Don't go any further until this passage is integrated into you." Here's what it says: "Then Jesus said to His twelve disciples, 'With My authority and power, go cast out demons, cure diseases, proclaim the Kingdom of God and heal the sick.'"

Okay. That sure looks a lot different than what I'd been taught to do in my discipleship follow-up course: spend time each morning reading Scripture and praying, join a church, give money to it, and witness with the four spiritual laws.

I imagined the disciples saying, "Jesus, aren't You coming with us? You expect us to do those things? No, don't you remember? You are the One who does the miracles; we are there to watch You do them." But Jesus was not to be deterred. He went further and told them, "When you go on your mission trip, two by two, don't take any luggage or credit cards with you." I don't know about you, but I think I would have been typing my resignation letter about then.

The light bulb went on for me. *The two hands were separating Church and Kingdom.* Institutional church in the building was my past; my future involved discovering what Jesus spoke in His Sermon on the Mount: "Seek first My Kingdom."

I wish I could say that after that realization, life got easier. Sadly, I felt like Moses after they crossed over the Red Sea. It didn't take long for the Israelites to forget the miracle and start to rewrite their memory of Egypt. Suddenly, their lives of slavery didn't seem so bad.

> *I knew I was supposed to be leading us differently, but after a lifetime of church attendance, I was having a hard time envisioning how it should look.*

One Sunday in early March, all those who had committed to become part of Missio Lux (the new church plant) stood before our mother church as they blessed us to go. The excitement amongst us was palpable; we were heading towards our promise land. The only problem was that none of us had a map for how to get there!

God had given me a plan that involved the finances, how we were to structure our monthly rhythms, and how each missio community could discern their missional purpose, but there were so many areas where I just had no idea what to do. Even my study of Scripture didn't lend too many clues because I was still reading it through the lens of church, rather than the illusive Kingdom Jesus pointed to over and over throughout His earthly ministry.

One piece of good news is that I don't lack courage. Those who came with me to discover life as a missional church were adventurous too, so we started walking and meeting and listening to the Lord for our direction. The monthly rhythm we designed in Missio Lux was to spend two weeks connecting in our missio communities, one week engaging our missional purpose, and one week gathering corporately as Missio Lux in a worship service.

But those who had excitedly come with me on this unknown journey suddenly found the same discomfort I had when we gathered to worship corporately just one time per month. I found out through the grapevine that many of them were continuing to go to our mother church on Sunday mornings, creating great confusion within our sending church. I understood. I felt the same level of confusion and disorientation.

As time went by, I kept hitting up against my past experience in the church. I knew I was supposed to be leading us differently, but after a lifetime of church attendance, I was having a hard time envisioning how it should look.

One day after a lot of wrestling with God and challenging conversations with the Missio Lux team, I found myself sobbing on my friend's floor, crying out to God, "Please God, it's [the church way] in my pores. The only way for me to lead differently is for You to remove it from my pores, so I can see the different way."

In the midst of my cry, my friend began to read John 21 aloud. "Friends, do you have any fish?" said the unknown man on the beach. Simon Peter, Thomas, Nathaniel, John, and Andrew, and two unnamed disciples dejectedly said, "No, not one fish after fishing all night." The mysterious man said, "Throw your nets to the right side of the boat." Exhausted, weary, and discouraged, they heaved the nets out—*opposite of the way they had ALWAYS been trained to do it*. Suddenly, their arms began to shake as they realized the weight of the nets. They were loaded with fish!

> ### *The way to lead was to follow the unfamiliar instructive to throw my nets to the right side of the boat.*

It was in the midst of that fishy miracle that Peter realized that the only one who could load nets with fish like that was Jesus. He threw on his tunic and jumped out of the boat (leaving his good and forgiving friends to haul in the fish) and ran to the One he knew loved him—Jesus, the greatest fisherman of all.

Suddenly, I got it. I'd been trying to continue to fish from the left-hand side of the boat just like I'd experienced and been trained all of my life.

The way to lead Missio Lux was to follow the unfamiliar instructive to throw my nets to the right side of the boat. It didn't change everything all of the sudden, but it did make a difference. Things that felt confusing and hard got easier to envision and implement.

> *Suddenly, I realized Jesus had given me a Kingdom compass, and the direction He wanted me to go was up to be with Him.*

I began to have glimmers of understanding that there doesn't have to be a dichotomy between church and the unbelieving community. A third way existed—the way of the Kingdom, the way of Jesus, following His unorthodox instruction. I even began to understand in a clearer way why getting "the boot" out of my familiar circumstances in the church building enabled me to discover a new language with different practices—the ways of the King in His Kingdom of Heaven established on earth.

Suddenly, I realized Jesus had given me a Kingdom compass, and the direction He wanted me to go was up to be with Him.

REFLECT

- Consider a time when you've been in disequilibrium. Perhaps a move, a new job, or becoming a parent. Remember how it felt. What did you do to find your balance and equilibrium again?

- Have you ever been lost? Where were you? What did you do to find your way through to where you were headed?

DO SOMETHING

- Do something different. Take a couple of Sundays off from church. Go out and see where people are. Start a conversation with them about what they do on Sunday mornings.

CHAPTER 3

BUT, GOD, IT DOESN'T LOOK LIKE ANYTHING

Leading Missio Lux was the hardest thing I've ever done. People began to get a vision for how they'd like to shape a missio community. We suddenly found that we had communities of people from South Korea, the Netherlands, and Abu Dhabi. Our communities' missional purposes all looked quite different. Some organized around a life stage, a geographical region, a people group, or ministry to the poor or disenfranchised. Some focused on healing and started a Celebrate Recovery and a healing prayer ministry. We started a nonprofit to equip future leaders of South Sudan through educating orphans from the Kakuma Refugee Camp. Even a ballet school was birthed.

I often felt like I was playing a ping pong game because of the vast range of leadership skills it took, causing my brain to bounce back and forth, but that wasn't the hardest part. The most challenging was envisioning what our monthly corporate gatherings should include. Each month, we would evaluate. We realized we were still far from our goal of a spontaneous gathering where we each told our stories and connected with one another. It wasn't focused on professional pastors who held the stage and had the only voice that mattered.

I wish I could say we got it right. I wish I could say that our fishing from the right side of the boat suddenly made it all clear and simple, but

I can't. It's hard to create something new from what we've never experienced. People began to slip away in disillusionment. They didn't think it would be so hard to lead a missio community. They came up against their own challenges and found it easier to go back to what was familiar—an organized church in a building where they could show up and have it all prepared for them.

> *We realize the best part of our day was sitting around the big table where we knew we belonged and our voice mattered.*

I liked to describe the difference this way: a comparison between *fine dining* and a *family dinner* around the kitchen table. To attend a worship service is much like choosing a fancy restaurant for Valentine's Day where we know that we will be served a delicious meal and be doted upon by an attentive server. We expect to pay for our meal, and we don't expect to chat with the other diners around us. We leave feeling satisfied from our delicious meal and continue to connect with our date.

Life in Missio Lux was more like a family meal around the kitchen table. Someone has to plan the meal, shop for the food, and prepare the menu. We all sit down, several people chatting at once, because we have so much to share. The food passes around and we eat, feeling blessed and satisfied because we are connecting with those whom we love and care for. The reality is when the meal is over, someone has to clear the table, wash the dishes, and put the leftovers away. There's a big element of work involved. But when we go home, we realize the best part of our day was sitting around the big table where we knew we belonged and our voice mattered.

One year, we held an Ash Wednesday service in our home. A new family came; their kids were around six and eight. They were enthralled! When they went home, they asked their parents more about Jesus, and that night, both of their children made decisions to follow Jesus. Their parents were ecstatic to see such growth in their kids. The kids had never been exposed to a service like they attended because they went to Sunday School at their mega church while their parents went to the worship service.

I fully expected the family would see the value in what they had experienced, and that they would take a next step with Missio Lux. Sadly, as I met with the mother, she told me, "No offense, but Missio Lux doesn't seem like a real church, so we won't be joining in." I wondered to myself, What is a church? I thought it was when people experienced Jesus' presence and became transformed through their experience. Obviously, these parents had different expectations, and their box for God seemed too small to embark on the journey of the King's Kingdom.

> *I wondered to myself, What is a church? I thought it was when people experienced Jesus' presence and became transformed through their experience.*

Our healing prayer ministry began to do quite a bit of prayer walking. We would listen for God to direct us to where strongholds existed, and we would move out in faith to follow Scripture's example in 2 Corinthians 10:3-5 where we are called to wage war with God's mighty weapons:

> *We are human, but we don't wage war with human plans and methods. We use God's mighty weapons, not mere worldly weapons, to knock down the Devil's strongholds. With these weapons we break down every proud argument that keeps people from knowing God. With these weapons we conquer their rebellious ideas, and we teach them to obey Christ.*

After several months of this, something began to change in our area. It was called "The Plateau" because our whole community was up on a big hill. Up to that point, churches were struggling because the affluent culture kept people busy and preoccupied away from spiritual pursuit. However, after several months of prayer walking, suddenly many people—especially men, husbands, and fathers—began to discover Jesus and His invitation to follow Him and began to take their families to church. The only problem was that none of them became part of Missio Lux!

I wish I could say that I was happy about it; that I celebrated all the growth that the primarily mega churches were experiencing, but I started to become angry and bitter and would complain to God about the situation. One day, I woke up and the first words out of my mouth were, "But God, Missio Lux doesn't look like anything." Then I sensed God's reply, "That is exactly the point."

Another big, "Huh? I don't get it. Why would You want me to put all this effort into developing something that looks invisible to the outside world?" Once again, I wish I could say I got it at that moment. Mostly, I was just more confused and frustrated. If we do the work, shouldn't we get credit for the fruit?

REFLECT

- Have you ever worked on or created something that another took the credit for? How did you feel?

- Consider this thought: You can change the trajectory of history if you are willing to be invisible. What does that bring up for you?

DO SOMETHING

- Watch the movie, *Pay It Forward*. (Or, if you've seen it, remember the concept of paying it forward.)

- Make a conscious plan to pay it forward. Practice it for one week. Observe your thoughts and feelings as you do it.

CHAPTER 4

NEW PRACTICES FOR NEW SEASONS

The amount of work I had with Missio Lux was staggering. I used to have a love-hate relationship with email. I called it "Email Jail" because at the end of a long day of mentoring leaders, meeting community representatives, and joining in a missio community or two, a long list of emails always awaited me.

But I was determined. I believed that if I worked hard, I would see results—people and communities would be transformed. I had no reason to doubt my assumption; it's what I learned in seminary, what I saw modeled to me by my church co-workers, as well as my heroes of faith in the larger Christian realm.

One day, out of sheer exhaustion, I cried out, "Lord, I just can't work any harder." I thought I would hear Him say back, "Yes, you can, with My strength you can do all things." But He didn't. He said, "Good, can we do it My way now instead?"

His way? I thought I was doing it His way. I spent a long time in prayer each morning, I studied the Scriptures and sought to follow them, and I invited many voices to speak into my life. The only problem was that I was interpreting all of it through *the lens of Christianity* instead of the Kingdom.

As the Lord continued to lead me to study the Scriptures about His Kingdom, I discovered some interesting things. The biggest was that the priorities of His Kingdom are upside down in comparison to the ways of 21st-century Christianity. Jesus' first use of the term "kingdom" is found in Mark 1:15, "The time has come. The Kingdom of God is near. Repent of your sins and believe the good news." I love *The Message Bible* that states, *"Time's up! God's kingdom is here. Change your life and believe the Message."*

> *One day, out of sheer exhaustion, I cried out, "Lord, I just can't work any harder." He said, "Good, can we do it My way now instead?"*

I pondered that Scripture for a long time. If it was Jesus' opening statement, it had to have significant priority to His message. I understood His statement, "The time has come." It had come because He was present in the world, but when I reflected on "Time's up," it meant that a change of season had come—a change of season from all that was known in the ways of living out faith.

In Jesus' day, the box was for the Jewish people to worship in the Temple. However, it had a certain way of access. Everyone was welcome in the outermost courtyard, even Gentiles. Jewish women could go no further than the women's courtyard. Jewish men could take a step deeper into the Temple courtyard, but only the priests could enter the sanctuary. The high priest was the only one who could enter the Holy of Holies and only once per year at that.

When Jesus came, He had a big box and invited a lot of unacceptable people to come around Him. He sought out the disenfranchised: the tax collectors, lepers, and prostitutes, the sick and the lame. He didn't tell them they didn't belong. Instead, He invited them to experience the Kingdom, very often through miracles that left them astonished.

I began to wonder. That is when Jesus told me not to read any further in the Bible until Luke 9:1-2 became part of my daily life: casting out demons, curing diseases, proclaiming the Kingdom of God, and healing the sick. Then He kicked me out of the familiar box of the church building to go do it.

I needed to understand that I was walking out a *kairos* moment of time (where God breaks through in a new way). It was imperative that I take a big step back and follow the invitation to discover God's Kingdom ways, so I could align my life with it and believe and act within Jesus' good news.

I used to be afraid of the word "repent." I thought it was a big and scary word that meant that I needed to fall on my face in sorrow, put on sackcloth, and rub ashes all over my face. In actuality, the word "repent" means to have a change of direction as we align with the highest thinking. God's way and His word are the highest thinking. Again, *The Message* says it so well: *"Time's up! God's kingdom is here. Change your life and believe the Message."*

I recently heard a speaker who took us on a tour through the different seasons of the Bible. I was fascinated when he got to the season in which we are currently living—*the transition between the Church Season and the Kingdom Age.* I suddenly had a huge realization. In the transition between seasons, much confusion abounds because what we are used to identifying or experiencing as success no longer works in creating transformation.

> *In the transition between seasons, much confusion abounds because what we are used to identifying or experiencing as success no longer works in creating transformation.*

Remember Zechariah, the father of John the Baptist? He was the priest who was chosen by lot to minister in the Holy of Holies. The angel Gabriel appeared and started talking to him (Luke 1:8-17). He was absolutely dumbfounded; in fact, he was shaken and overwhelmed with fear. I've always wondered why it was such a surprise. What better place to encounter an angel than in the Holy of Holies? But remember, the Israelites had not experienced anything supernatural breaking through for over 400 years. Zechariah was firmly planted in the season he'd been living his entire life.

It gets better. Angel Gabriel quotes Malachi to him, the very last passage of the Old Testament. It's my bet that because Zechariah was a priest, he knew the words in Malachi really well; he may have even had them memorized: *"Look, I am sending you the prophet Elijah before the great and dreadful day of the Lord arrives. His preaching will turn the hearts of parents to their children, and the hearts of children to their parents"* (Malachi 4:5-6).

Zechariah was utterly flabbergasted. Gabriel was telling him that after decades of waiting, they were to have a son. He would come in the spirit and power of Elijah. However, even after encountering the angel in the Holy of Holies, Zechariah was so firmly planted in his season that he couldn't embrace in faith what he was being told. His box was simply too small.

> *Just as Jesus created massive upheaval with His arrival on earth, we are experiencing the earthquake of the full arrival of the King's Kingdom.*

He asked a question which came out of doubt and fear: "How can I know for sure this will happen?" He looked at his *earthly circumstances*—both Zechariah and Elizabeth were old—rather than his *heavenly opportunity*. This didn't make Angel Gabriel very happy; in fact, he offered him a strong rebuke and then silenced Zechariah, so he couldn't make any more doubting statements.

It's easy to criticize Zechariah 2,000 years later, but the reality is that we are a lot like him. We become so entrenched in our daily spiritual practices that when something new takes place, we are often more likely to shut it down then to fully embrace it. The box of comfort is a strong motivator.

I know it's true for me. I had my spiritual practices down. They were even fulfilling me, but when God showed up and kicked me out of the church building and then proceeded to tell me that my new course of action was Luke 9:1-2 (casting out demons, curing diseases, healing the sick, and preaching about the Kingdom), I felt more confused than anything. At times, I even felt angry. Why would we disrupt something that was going so well?

I find it interesting that the book of Revelation begins with seven letters to seven churches, but in chapter four, an abrupt change takes place. Revelation 4:1 begins with an invitation: *"I saw a door standing open in heaven, and the same voice I had heard before spoke to me with the sound of a trumpet blast. The voice said, 'Come up here, and I will show you what must happen after these things.'"*

Suddenly, John was called to exercise new spiritual practices which involved seeing with spiritual eyes and hearing with spiritual ears. He was called into *experience* rather than a *belief system*. The rest of Revelation isn't for the faint of heart; it challenges just about every preconception he must have held.

This describes me too. For almost 10 years, the Lord has been teaching me new spiritual practices that are very different from how I was trained and taught or modeled in the first few decades of my Christian life. They continue to stretch me, taking me down to my knees in dependence on Holy Spirit, causing me to ask God to show me a different measuring system, to show me if I am on the right track.

I believe that we are in a huge place of confusion, dissatisfaction, frustration, and even fear because we are walking out the transition between the long-term season of Church and the age of Kingdom. Just as Jesus created massive upheaval with His arrival on earth, we are experiencing the earthquake of the full arrival of the King's Kingdom.

It's time to stop and re-orient ourselves to this new season.

REFLECT

Have you ever felt like God directed you to do something that was outside of your lens or comfort zone? How did you respond? What did you feel as a result?

DO SOMETHING

- What's your rhythm for meeting with God? When, where, and what do you do?

- Consider shaking it up and doing something very different. Reflect on what happened to you as a result? (Don't be hard on yourself if you didn't like the shift; you'll be in good company, as transition always has an element of challenge.)

CHAPTER 5

NAVIGATING TRANSITIONS

I never realized how much Jesus spoke about His Kingdom until I entered into my journey of transitioning out of the Church Season and into the Kingdom Age. As I pointed out before, it was the first declaration of His ministry (Mark 1:15). It is the big idea of His Sermon on the Mount, which I believe is an accumulation of His core teachings (Matthew 5-7). It is the declaration of His teaching on prayer: *"Thy Kingdom come"* (Matthew 6:10). It is His call to action: "Seek the Kingdom of God above all else, and live righteously, and He will give you everything you need" (Matthew 6:33). It is the guidebook for direction: *"You can enter God's Kingdom only through the narrow gate"* (Matthew 7:13).

It is also what led Jesus to His death. We see Jesus' disciples struggling to understand what He is saying because their paradigm was rooted in the hope of the Messiah's coming to set the Israelites free from their oppression from the Romans and to restore the Kingdom to its glory days from King Solomon's reign. It is the reason Judas ended up betraying Him; he wasn't seeing Jesus boldly move towards reclaiming the throne. He knew it was a losing cause when Jesus entered Jerusalem on a donkey rather than a majestic horse.

I don't think Judas intended for Jesus to die. He just wanted to give Jesus a wake-up call to remind Him of the mission ahead, so that as He experienced Rome's oppression, He would be ready to whip out the swords and then gather other revolutionaries who would seize the day to reclaim the throne.

I find it interesting that those closest to Jesus missed Him so fully. After Jesus left His 40 days of desert training, the first place He went was into the synagogue in which He grew up (Luke 4:17-30). He made His missional declaration out of Isaiah 61. Everything was going well; His friends and family were utterly amazed. But then two pivotal events took place. The spirit of familiarity came over the congregation. They turned to one another and said, "Isn't this Joseph's son, the one we've known since he was young?" The second is that Jesus didn't stop while He was ahead. He proceeded to speak to them about how no prophet is accepted in His hometown, and how God sent Elijah to the Gentiles over the Jews.

We know the story, the crowd got so angry that they tried to kill Him by pushing Him off a cliff. Here's what I didn't realize for a long time: The mob trying to kill Jesus were His friends and family, the ones He'd known all His life. Pretty risky, especially because at that point in His ministry, He didn't have even one disciple or follower.

> *The mob trying to kill Jesus were His friends and family, the ones He'd known all His life.*

I always thought that Jesus' family must have known about His special birth and status. But I guess not because we find in John 7:3-5 that Jesus' brothers taunted Him by saying, "Why are You hanging out in this no name place, Nazareth? When are You going up to Jerusalem for Your followers to see Your great miracles? You can't become famous if You hide like this!" John ends by saying, *"Even His brothers didn't believe in Him."*

We also know Jesus didn't win any popularity contests with the Pharisees and Sadducees. What we may forget, however, is the enormous amount of influence they carried in their culture. People were terrified of being put out of their local synagogue because without it, they became persona non grata—they would be socially, vocationally, and spiritually ostracized.

Amazingly, the men most prepared by training and vocation to recognize the Messiah ended up being the ones who sent Him to His death.

Curiously, it was the disciples who spent three years in day-to-day training with Jesus, who had the most exposure to Him after His resurrection but still weren't clear about the reality of Jesus' mission. Acts 1 informs us that Jesus spent His 40 days on earth talking to them about the Kingdom of God, but they were so entrenched in their thinking that the Messiah would restore the Kingdom of Israel to its glory days, that even as He prepared to ascend into heaven, they asked the question again, *"Lord, has the time now come for You to free Israel and restore our kingdom?"* (Acts 1:6).

> *Amazingly, the men most prepared by training and vocation to recognize the Messiah ended up being the ones who sent Him to His death.*

In seasons of transition—such as the one we are currently experiencing between the Church Season and the Kingdom Age—it is vital that we hold our opinions loosely because what was true yesterday may take us in a direction exact opposite of where we intend to go.

Remember Peter? He fell asleep on a roof and was given a new menu of meat to eat. Not to worry, Peter knew the rules; he'd followed them all his life, so he quickly responded by telling the Lord, "I know they are forbidden; I won't disobey you by eating them" (Acts 10). But he was rebuked for his answer. The voice said, "Don't call something unclean if God has made it clean." Whoa, that's a switch!

We're told that Peter was perplexed. That's a huge understatement. Don't you think he was experiencing the disorientation that comes from having your entire life thrown up into the sky to see what will fall down first? Peter didn't have to wait long; just minutes later, three Gentile men came looking for him to invite him to the home of a Gentile named Cornelius, who had invited all his friends and family to hear Peter.

Peter, being the extrovert that he was, stated the cultural reality by telling them, "You know that it's against Jewish law for a Jewish man to enter into a Gentile home. *But God* has shown me that I should no longer think of anyone as impure or unclean."

His head must have been spinning. Fortunately for us, Peter made a quick transition and went to Cornelius' house because this was the first experience of Gentiles meeting Jesus and experiencing the Holy Spirit being poured out on them. They even got baptized. In a moment, those who had always been ostracized were now enfolded into God's heart.

These situations should give us pause as we walk through this challenging period of history. When we form our opinions and practices around what is common and known and continue to use them to guide us through transition, *our own lens* can actually lead us away from God's purposes and heart.

> ### *Our own lens can actually lead us away from God's purposes and heart.*

Our opportunity in this massive historical transition is to learn to recognize God's voice in a deeper way as He, as loving Father, guides us into new ideas and practices. It is an opportunity to discover Jesus as King of the Universe, beyond how we've known Him as Savior and Messiah. It is an opportunity to depend on Holy Spirit as our guide, so He can open up new ideas and doors for us to walk through. It's an opportunity for our boxes around God to be dismantled and for us to know Him in a whole new way.

Yes, there is a cost. It is the same cost Jesus paid—to be misunderstood, to be challenged by the religious authorities, and ultimately, at times, even to be killed. But here's the flipside of the cost: "Without a vision, people perish" (Proverbs 29:18). If we continue to believe and do the same things during this massive transition, we just may shrivel up and die from lack of vision, movement, and breath.

REFLECT

- Have you experienced a restlessness or dissatisfaction with your current faith practices? Where do you think this is coming from?

- Great numbers of people accept Jesus as their "personal savior." Many follow Him as their "Lord." Fewer partner with Him as "King." Where are you in your faith maturity? How well do you know Jesus as the King of the Universe?

- What might He be inviting you to experience with Him as King?

DO SOMETHING

- Spend time worshipping in Revelation 4. Imagine the open door to heaven and then walk through it. What did you experience?

CHAPTER 6

THE SHOOTS OF HOPE

I thought that leading Missio Lux was my destiny. I had good reason to believe that. It had such a miraculous start, and everywhere we went as a team, we were given prophetic words and promises that were breathtaking. I guess I can say that I am a lot like Abraham. I believe God, so I kept those promises in my heart and trusted they would come to pass.

After four years of walking out Missio Lux and at the beginning of the new year, we had a week of prayer where we gathered each morning and evening to pray. Overwhelmingly, the theme we received was that we were being called to a season of rest. We envisioned that many of our challenges would get easier, the missio communities would experience breakthroughs, and our circle of connection would enlarge.

Were we ever wrong! We continued to experience extremely challenging situations that seemed bigger than us. Discouragement continued to grow as the missional dreams that spurred us forward began to fade away to nothingness. I continued to work really hard, getting to the point where my family expressed concern for my health and well-being. The word "rest" seemed to be a big joke from God.

Our leadership team recognized that our central core wasn't strong enough to support our missional activity. Too often it fell back on me. We prayed and sought the Lord for how we were to move differently. We tried the traditional route of seeking to hire admins, but something always blocked their ability to start. We tried creative approaches. No go. We begged some of our missional activists to come and share in the administrative load. It seemed that no matter what we did, the situation just got worse and worse. I began to feel desperate.

At the same time, our marriage began to struggle. My husband was commuting full time from Seattle to San Francisco, so I could be faithful to fulfill my call to lead Missio Lux. But by the time he came in the door Friday evenings, staggering from exhaustion, I had nothing left with which to greet him, as I was also weary and stressed. It became unworkable for us to be separated during the week. We needed to make an adjustment, but no matter how we framed it, we didn't see a clear solution for change.

Finally, that summer, I went to San Francisco to stay with Bill for a month while I finished writing *Identity Crisis: Reclaim the True You.* It was our time together that made it clear that something drastic needed to happen. Bill's company made the decision for us. They told him that they would no longer support his commuting. I needed to move with him to California.

Remember, I still had big dreams, so I saw it as opportunity. I would go to California and begin to pioneer Missio Lux in Northern California, while those in Seattle and in other continents would continue their missio communities. It was a big goal, but we had big faith and believed God would support us through the transition. What I didn't realize at the time was how close to a breakdown I was due to sheer exhaustion.

One morning three months after we moved to California, out of the blue, I sensed God say, "You need a spiritual hospital." I wondered aloud, What's a spiritual hospital? I didn't have to wait long because a couple of days later, I got a picture in prayer of me being in one of those army tents where the wounded and sick would go during the world wars. I was bruised, battered, and beaten from head to toe. It made me gasp to realize it was me!

Then this message came clear: "This is a picture of the hits you've taken for Missio Lux as you and your team have pioneered breakthrough in the spiritual realm. You need to rest and recover."

Within 48 hours, the message that I needed to take a sabbatical came to me in every creative way that you can imagine. I knew it couldn't be denied, so I called the leader of our transition team and told her the news.

She agreed, and within the week, all the arrangements were made for me to take a few months off to rest and recover. She would lead the team in discovering how to strengthen the center core, so it could support the missional activity.

I sensed God say, "You need a spiritual hospital."

I went into the sabbatical with a knowing that Missio Lux was at a tender place, and that it may not make it through its current season. Thankfully, the transition team was determined to find the answer to our dilemma. They worked really hard during that season, putting all their focus on the core challenge. The only problem was that they became so focused on the center core that leadership within the missional communities suffered, which caused the communities to struggle.

When I was finally released to resume leadership, I discovered that Missio Lux was on life support. It was obvious that we needed to close. I was heartbroken. I kept asking the Lord, "What about Your promises? I am like Abraham; I believed You."

At one point, I was in so much pain that I decided to go upstairs to our blue bedroom, creatively called the "Blue Room," to be blue and wrestle it out with God. I took my Bible, my journal, and a pitcher of water and committed to stay until I understood what God was doing. As I sat down on the bed, the sobs came and consumed me. In between them, however, I kept crying out, "I trust you, Father. I trust you." I didn't want to give away anything else to our common enemy, the devil.

That night I didn't sleep much as I continued to wrestle, seeking to understand how this supernaturally-birthed ministry could end up looking like it did. Other than leaving my husband a note (he was taking a nap at the time), no one knew I had made the climb into my upper room except one woman who prayed for me. I sent her a text that said, "My soul is anguished to the point of death."

Eventually, the Lord took me to Hebrews 11, and I began to understand what was taking place. There's a repetitive theme in Hebrews 11:

Verse 13—All these people died still believing what God had promised them. They did not receive what was promised, but they saw it from a distance and welcomed it.

Verse 16—They were looking for a better place, a heavenly homeland. That is why *"God is not ashamed to be called their God, for He has prepared a city for them"* (NKJV)

Verse 39—All these people earned a good reputation because of their faith, yet none of them received all that God had promised.

That morning, my friend, who knew nothing beyond my text, called me. She said, "The Lord wants you to know that a space has been made in heaven by Missio Lux for future generations to walk through." That was a confirmation. God *is* fulfilling His promises and prophecies. We just may not see the fullness of it in our lifetime on earth.

> *I knew that my earthly circumstances didn't determine my heavenly identity.*

When I was finished being blue in the Blue Room with God, I knew that I had put some stakes in the ground of my faith. First, I trusted the ways, heart, and purposes of my Heavenly Father. I didn't understand what He was doing, but I was choosing with my will to trust Him. Secondly, I knew that my earthly circumstances didn't determine my heavenly identity. It may have looked like everything was falling apart around me, but heaven had a different measurement. Finally, I knew that I still had a call to equip God's people and to lead them into transformational breakthrough. I didn't know what it would look like from there, but I knew that my call still mattered.

I wish I could say that everything magically corrected itself from there, but I still had to walk through laying down Missio Lux and facing the disappointment of the core community, our sending church, and our denomination.

> **God isn't worried about failure nearly as much as He cares about our faithfulness.**

However, I did get peace at the end of my wrestling. I learned something in the Blue Room: God values our faith and trust much more than any type of success we may be pursuing. He isn't worried about failure nearly as much as He cares about our faithfulness.

Weeks continued to go by, often accompanied with painful conversations and situations. One weekend, my sister-in-law came to visit, and we made plans to go to Armstrong Woods, a beautiful forest of majestic redwood trees. Right before we left, I read an email that created another pang in my spirit, so I entered into the forest with a very heavy heart.

All the while we walked through the majestic trees, I kept crying out, "Lord, what's the point? Why does Missio Lux need to die?" It had been my mantra through the summer. I was still confused about why He would choose that path for something that held so much promise.

He answered me that day with the description of a fairy circle. It was explained that before a tree died, it would send out shoots in a circle that would become new trees. Then the Lord said, "Tamara, here's the point. Missio Lux, as an *organization*, is giving its life, so that the shoots that come from it will not only survive but also thrive and go on to significantly impact My Kingdom."

Suddenly, I got it! It was never about the organization. When we made maintaining the organization the point and the focus, we were going in the wrong direction. It was time for the Lord to intervene and show us what He could do in the midst of destruction. I left my heavy heart in the redwood forest and exchanged it for a heart of joy. Once I understood the point, I could walk it out with confidence.

So, I took steps forward. I scheduled a date to go back to Seattle and lead a time of closure. I called the church planting leader in our denomination and gave him our news. He didn't berate me for failure but graciously stated, "You were faithful and courageous, and much has been learned through it." Wow! What I thought would be a rebuke became a blessing.

> *I left my heavy heart in the redwood forest and exchanged it for a heart of joy.*

When our mother church knew I was coming, they asked me to say a few words about Missio Lux's closure. That morning in my hotel bathroom, I sensed the Lord inviting me to share with them His presence with me in the wilderness. As I shared about my journey walking through the wilderness and God's faithful presence through it, my heart got lighter. When I talked about my encounter in the redwood forest with the fairy circle, I got a standing ovation. After the service was over, a long line of people formed with each person telling me how I had helped equip them to become shoots from the redwood tree.

After the church service, I proceeded to our closure gathering with the Missio Lux team. We looked back and told stories of how we'd seen God's love and power arise within us. We grieved the loss of something so dear to us. At the end, I passed out "shoots" along with unveiling a dying tree. I invited each person present to bring their shoot, so that together we would create a circle around the dying stump while each person declared what their shoot would be.

As each person stood to make their declaration, hope began to emerge in the room. Suddenly, we realized we were moving from crucifixion and death into resurrection By the time we finished, we had released seeds of faith that were being planted into the soil of God's Kingdom. Each one of us entered into our closure service with sadness and grief, but God took our emotions and resurrected each one of us into a "shoot of hope" that would go forth, not just to survive, but to fully thrive and to significantly impact His Kingdom.

As I drove out of the city in the early morning hours the next day, I realized that what should have been one of the hardest, most devastating days of my life had become one of my greatest days of blessings from God. Only a miraculous, resurrecting God can accomplish a feat like that!

REFLECT

- Remember a time when something you believe God promised you went the other way towards death. How did you respond?

- Considering the new lens of Hebrews 11, is there another way to discern what could have been happening?

DO SOMETHING

- Study redwood fairy circles/rings. http://crosstalk.cell.com/blog why-redwoods-are-one-of-the-great-wonders-of-the-world

- Consider the concept along with Jesus' statement, "I tell you the truth, unless a kernel of wheat is planted in the soil and dies, it remains alone. But its death will produce many new kernels—a plentiful harvest of new lives" (John 12:24). Where have you experienced this? Bring your broken dreams and hopes to the Lord and allow Him to breathe new life into them, bringing forth a harvest!

CHAPTER 7

THE KINGDOM IS NEITHER HERE NOR THERE

Have you ever tried to hold water in your hands? When I'd walk my beloved Bernese Mountain Dog in California, she'd get really hot. To help her, I'd pour out water from my bottle into my hands, so she could drink. After a couple of laps, I'd see the majority of my water spilled out on the ground. Water goes where it wants to go, no matter what we want it to do.

The tricky thing about the Kingdom of God is that it's like water in our hands. It doesn't stay in them; it goes where it wants to go. How do we describe the Kingdom? It's the King's Kingdom on earth. But where's the throne? Where's the capitol? Where's the sign announcing it? What does it look like practically?

The Pharisees wanted the answer. They showed up to ask Jesus the latest question of the week in Luke 17:20. "Jesus, when will the Kingdom of God arrive?" I guess they figured since He kept talking about it, they wanted to know when they could sign up. Jesus didn't make it any easier for them. He was quick to tell them, *"The Kingdom of God isn't ushered in with visible signs. You won't be able to say, 'Here it is!' or 'It's over there.' For the Kingdom of God is already among you."*

Well, that's helpful. It sure wasn't going to compete with the majestic Temple in Jerusalem that took decades and a boatload of money to build.

After all, it was the sterling representation of Jewish faith and culture. They not only worshipped *in* the Temple; they worshipped *the Temple.*

> ### The tricky thing about the Kingdom of God is that it's like water in our hands.

Now, Jesus comes along and tells the people, you can't pin down the Kingdom. You can't subject it to doctrinal conversations or interrogations. You certainly can't sell birds and animals for sacrifice from something invisible. And even worse, if it doesn't have defined boundaries, what keeps the "socially unacceptable" from entering?

I stopped calling myself a Christian a long time ago. I realized that Christianity had become more of a cultural declaration than a statement of relationship. I now describe myself as a Kingdom seeker. When asked to describe what that means, I still find myself trying to describe it. I know that my first priority every day is to follow Jesus' instruction to seek first His Kingdom and live in right alignment with its ways (Matthew 6:33).

The challenge is that the Kingdom is still so elusive. It doesn't have a headquarters, a belief statement, or a membership roster. It's also invisible. Right when I think I've found it or can describe it, it disappears.

We recently moved to Denver from California. The first time my daughter and I went to look for a grocery store, we passed by one huge church after another. We counted seven churches by the time we found food to purchase. I was dumbfounded. After living on the West Coast for 14 years in Seattle and Sonoma County, I wasn't used to seeing so many churches, especially the size found on the church row I now regularly travel going to the more sparsely numbered grocery stores.

There's no question if they are visible. They are all positioned with big signs and giant parking lots. They have active websites, Facebook pages, and podcasts of their sermons. It makes one wonder if "church" isn't about getting the best preacher, worship leader, or website designer. With today's mass promotion and motto of "out of sight, out of mind," it's nearly impossible for a church to understand, and even greater, to embrace the Kingdom principle of being invisible.

Even though Jesus announced that the Kingdom of God was among the Jewish people, *not one person* ever publicly acknowledged His kingly presence, that is, until He met His executioner. After Jesus was arrested, He was first taken to the Jewish leaders. They did not have the authority to put Him to death, so they took Him to their Roman governor, Pilate.

Interestingly, the first question Pilate asked Him was, *"Are you the King of the Jews?"* (John 18:33). He was the first person in Jesus' life to ever ask that question. Why? What did Pilate see that everyone else had missed?

Jesus answered him by asking the question, "Is this your question or did the Jewish leaders tell you I was their king?"

Pilate didn't answer; he only asked again, "What did you do to make the Jewish leaders so furious with you?"

Jesus didn't answer that question either but went to the heart of the Kingdom matter by stating, "My Kingdom is not an earthly kingdom. If it were, My followers would be fighting to keep Me from being handed over to the Jewish leaders. But My kingdom is not of this world" (John 18:36).

> *Pilate was the first person in Jesus' life to ever ask that question. Why? What did Pilate see that everyone else had missed?*

So, there is the dilemma. If Jesus was willing to fight for the earthly throne, His followers would have gotten their weapons ready and would have fought to the death, but because Jesus had a different priority—the upside-down way of the supernatural—He was alone. His followers not only didn't fight for Him, two of them betrayed Him. One led Him to His arrest and even death.

Amazingly, Pilate, a secular Roman governor, got it. He responded, "Oh, so you are a king?" This must be why Jesus told His followers, "You can enter God's Kingdom only through the narrow gate. The road to destruction is broad and its gate is wide for the many who choose that way. But, the gateway to life is very narrow and the road is difficult, so only a few will ever find it" (Matthew 7:13-14). Rarely in the Kingdom is the obvious path the one that will lead towards life.

Pilate tried to find a way out of executing Jesus. He designed a creative bargain, but the Jewish leaders were not to be deterred. They threatened to set Him up for His own arrest. Pilate gave it one more try. He brought Jesus to the judgment seat and yelled out, "Look! Here is your king!" (Mark 15:12).

I find this the most ironic of all, the Jewish leaders who were desperate to get out from under the rule and oppression of the Roman government declares, *"We have no king but Caesar"* (John 19:15). Finally, defeated, exhausted, and downright scared, Pilate reluctantly handed Jesus over to be crucified.

I am experiencing the same dichotomy today. My secular, unchurched friends have regular interactions with me regarding the King's Kingdom. They seem to come from a base of understanding that allows them to accept that it doesn't need to have a building, a budget, or a professional Christian leading the charge. But because we are new to Denver, the first question we are often asked by our Christian friends is "Where do you go to church?"

Where do I start? If I try to explain, their eyes often roll over, and they change the subject. If I say—which is the truth—"We haven't found one yet," they give me a look that I can't quite describe...confusion, annoyance, perhaps even judgment?

Because I think Pilate saw something in Jesus that everyone else missed, I believe he was determined to at least have Him die under His proper title. Posted above His cross in three languages, so *no one missed it,* was "Jesus of Nazareth, the King of the Jews." Behold the irony once again, Jesus' executioner was the only one who saw it...and he got the final word.

REFLECT

- Do you see any parallels to this chapter in our culture today? What perspective shift might happen if we step outside the system to see it?

- What do you think might be out of balance in today's religious culture?

DO SOMETHING

- Look, listen, and discern Kingdom seekers who may not be churched. Have a conversation with them and discover their hearts of faith. Where is it similar to yours? Where is it different?

CHAPTER 8

WE CAN'T THINK OUR WAY INTO THE KINGDOM

John the Baptist and Jesus were cousins. We know John and Jesus at least knew about one another because Jesus' mother, Mary, went to visit Elizabeth, John's mother, when she became pregnant. When Mary came into the house, the baby in Elizabeth's womb, John, leapt with joy.

Both mothers were in on the secret that Jesus' true identity was God's beloved Son rather than the son of his earthly dad, Joseph, as everyone else believed. So, it leads me to wonder, how much did Mary and Elizabeth say to their sons, Jesus and John? Did they reveal the other's identity to them? Did they tell them the story of their sacred weeks together while they were both pregnant?

We don't know the answer, but this we do know. When John the Baptist saw Jesus walking towards him, John knew that Jesus was the One he'd been talking about when he said to the crowds, *"I baptize you with water, but someone is coming soon who is greater than I am—so much greater that I am not even worthy to be his slave. He will baptize you with the Holy Spirit and with fire"* (Luke 3:16).

John also cried out, *"Behold the Lamb of God who takes away the sins of the world"* (John 1:29, NKJV). After his declaration, Jesus asked John the Baptizer to baptize Him, but John protested, "No, of course not, You should be the one baptizing me." But Jesus insisted, so John took Him into the water and baptized Him.

While Jesus was coming up out of the water, the Kingdom arrived. The Holy Spirit, in the form of a dove, flew down and landed on Jesus' head. Then a voice cried out from heaven, *"This is My beloved Son in whom I take great pleasure"* (Matthew 3:17).

Imagine what that moment must have been like to John as he had faithfully fulfilled his ministry call to cry out for repentance in God's favored people, the Jews, in preparation for the Messiah's arrival. Do you think he knew at that moment that his role was fulfilled? Possibly not. Shortly after Jesus' baptism, John the Baptist was arrested by Herod and put in prison. Eventually, Herod ordered John killed. I hope he died knowing he faithfully completed his calling.

But, when prison becomes your new address, you suddenly have time to think and wonder and ask questions. John was no exception, and eventually his crystal-clear perception became cloudy, and he began to question if he'd judged the situation with Jesus correctly. Finally, he could stand it no longer, and he sent his disciples to ask Jesus the million-dollar question, *"Are you the Messiah we've been waiting for or should we look for someone else?"* (Matthew 11:3).

> *Jesus focused on individuals, rather than on nations and rulers.*

Don't you wonder why he asked Jesus that question? What was Jesus doing or not doing that caused John to waiver and wonder? I think it all comes down to *where* he (and Jesus' disciples) thought Jesus' Kingdom would be established. John the Baptist had it wrong just like Jesus' disciples. They envisioned the Messiah's Kingdom as an earthly one, established *on earth* in Israel rather than a spiritual one established in the heart. They longed for the glory days of their past when Israel was at the top, rather than being the lowly subjects of Rome, oppressed religiously, politically, and economically.

One of the challenges for them was that Jesus kept giving power away, rather than grabbing hold of it. He told everyone that He didn't come to be served but to serve and to give away His life. His disciples and John the Baptist weren't sold on that philosophy. They wanted to have a part in the power that would come through Jesus, the long-awaited Messiah, reigning on the throne of Israel.

All Jesus' priorities were upside down to that dream. He sought out the poor, the disenfranchised, the basic losers of the culture, and made them His friends. He touched the untouchable lepers, so that He couldn't even enter into towns; people had to come out to the desert to find Him. He stopped funeral processions to minister to a broken-hearted mother. He healed an "unclean" woman who'd been bleeding for 12 years, making her once again clean and whole. *He focused on individuals, rather than on nations and rulers.*

His answer to John was simple, as it was based on His upside-down priorities: "Go back to John and point to the miracles: the blind can see, the lame can walk, the deaf can hear, the dead are even raised to life, and the good news is being preached to the poor" (Matthew 11:5). This isn't the message of a revolutionary ready to take over the world. This is the action of a quiet healer, who often tells those He heals not to reveal His true identity but to keep it to themselves.

Jesus concludes His answer to John's disciples with an intriguing statement: "Tell John, blessed are those who don't turn away because of Me." Here's the reality:

- We cannot *think* our way into the Kingdom. It doesn't work. It's not a rational Kingdom.
- We can't *intellectualize* our way into the Kingdom. It doesn't work. It's not an academic pursuit.
- We can't *explain* our way into the Kingdom. It doesn't work. It's not defined by words or theories.
- We can't *structure* our way into the Kingdom. It doesn't work. It's not defined by goals and objectives.
- We can't *posture* our way into the Kingdom. It doesn't work. The only power that is present in the Kingdom is supernatural power released from heaven.
- We can't box our way into the Kingdom. It doesn't work. Jesus is the master of ripping apart our boxes and unleashing the Kingdom.

I have a good friend named Ian. He's an unlikely friend because he is 20 years younger than me and he's a man, but we have a great relationship based on pursuing the King's Kingdom. He came to a retreat that I led a couple of years ago called "Reclaim Your Identity." At the end of the retreat, the participants would always make a reclamation presentation that highlighted how God had broken through in their lives.

On the final morning of the retreat, the participants began to present their reclamation projects. When we took a break, I realized Ian was nowhere to be found. Eventually, I found him pacing within our olive grove. I asked him if he was coming in to make his presentation, and he said no.

What was stopping him? He was tied up in knots by his attempt to *think*, *rationalize*, and *define* his way into the King's Kingdom, and he couldn't do it. He was in the middle of a big faith crisis, which caused him to bolt from the retreat before he had to own up to the other participants that he was breaking down and couldn't complete his reclamation project!

We met later to process the experience. I started out our conversation gently saying, "Ian, you can't think your way into the Kingdom. It's invisible. It's hard to define. But, it's real, and it changes you." Ian has five kids, all born before he turned 30. He's a great dad and nothing makes him happier than to be on the floor playing with them. As we sat together, I remembered one of the profound statements the King made about His Kingdom, "Unless you become like a little child, you cannot enter into the Kingdom of Heaven" (Matthew 18:3).

That truth spoke to Ian above all else. He gets little children. He welcomes them, too, just like Jesus did. Suddenly, the light bulb went on in Ian. He jumped up ready to embrace a totally different lifestyle—one of presence, one of joy, one of trust…just like small children have with their parents.

Apparently, Ian got the Kingdom quicker than the disciples because Matthew tells us that parents got the wonderful idea to have Jesus bless their children. They started bringing their kids to Him, so He could lay hands on them and pray for them (Matthew 19:13-15). But the disciples stood by and watched the clock tick by, thinking, looking, and resenting *all the time being wasted*. They thought, "These parents and kids aren't going to bring us closer to our revolutionary goal," so they tried to shoo them away.

But Jesus, in His upside-down Kingdom priorities, stopped His friends and invited the next child onto His lap. He stated emphatically, "Let the children come to Me. They get it...and for you to get it, you need to become like a child. In fact, the Kingdom of Heaven belongs to those who are just like these children."

Now, let me ask you, whose lap do you sit upon?

REFLECT

- Historically, we've been in a period of pursuing faith through our mind. Our culture is currently in a post-modern season, opening the door to experience and many diverse points of view. Where do you see strengths in this for the Christian faith? What does it threaten?

- What process have you used to live your faith? What would it look like for you to lay all that down and pursue the King's illusive Kingdom?

DO SOMETHING

- Worship to "Be Enthroned" by Jeremy Riddle.

CHAPTER 9

IN THE KINGDOM, EVERYONE GETS TO PLAY

I had an unlikely call to seminary. I went to a college that also had a seminary, and I was so determined that I didn't want to have anything to do with ministry, or even worse, become a pastor's wife, that I steered clear of all the seminary students, which was at times a big sacrifice because a couple of them were, well how should I say it...drop-dead handsome!

However, I had a passion for children, so when our kids were small, I was asked to become the Sunday School superintendent at our church. I said, "Yes," and went to town recruiting teachers and leaders for the kids. I must have been quite good at it because not long after, I was asked to apply to become the children's director as a paid position.

I loved that job. It made me so happy to discover the hidden gifts in the parents and congregants and then to call them into a role where they would be fulfilled. Suddenly, the children's volunteer roster was greater than the rest of the church put together.

I was so hungry to learn and grow that I kept asking the church to invest in me, so I could become better at what I did. I was usually told, "You are just the children's director. We need to send the pastors to trainings. Remember, we have limited funds." Of course, who was I to forget that I wasn't one of the "club"—the revered seminary-trained pastors.

Sometimes when I prayed, I would get ideas that would impact the whole church. I would try to share them but was once again told, "You are just the children's director. We have the rest of the church covered." Of course, I "just" led the children. Who was I to forget that I didn't carry the same status because I didn't have the invaluable seminary training?

So, I tried my best to stay in my corner, the children's department, and keep my overflowing ideas under wraps. But apparently, the Lord wasn't all that happy about the ways that I wasn't being equipped, heard, or honored for my gifting. I started to feel this presence behind me. At first, it just happened occasionally, but I would sense it saying, "You should go to seminary." I would shake my head and go back to what I was doing, but after a few months, it became quite the nag. I would feel it constantly, insistent that I hear the message, "You should go to seminary."

One day, it was so intense, I actually turned around and said, "Stop it! I am not going to seminary. I have no money for it. I don't know any women in seminary, and besides that, absolutely *no one* is encouraging me to go to seminary."

I thought that would be it, but apparently, the "nag" just took on the challenge. It became more and more insistent. Finally, I capitulated. I opened a savings account and began to put a few dollars into it. It was slow going because I made so little, and our family was young and money wasn't exactly growing on trees. Months went by. My new friend, now affectionately named "The Nag," continued to stay with me. Only once, when I opened the bank account, it moved to my side as a friend rather than talking behind my back!

One Christmas season, I was sitting in a MOPS (Mothers of Pre-Schoolers) brunch, listening to a rather boring speaker but feasting on the beautiful bulletin board that one of the parent volunteers had created. I was enjoying the moment, content with the world, when a new voice said, "Enjoy this. You aren't going to be here much longer."

I immediately said, "That's ridiculous, God. This is the church of my childhood; my family is here, we have a thousand friends here, and besides that, I just love my role as children's director." I quickly forgot about that word and didn't even note it in my journal where all my God thoughts got recorded.

A couple of months later, I was all alone in the church building in one of the Sunday School rooms, preparing for an event. Suddenly, the tangible presence of God filled up the room, and all these memories came flooding back to me: being taught lessons by my Sunday School teachers as a child, cutting my finger carving soap as a Brownie and bleeding all the way down the hall to the bathroom, filling up the room with helium balloons on Easter, and more. Then the voice spoke again, "You won't be here much longer."

I wondered, "Where will I go?" I didn't have to wonder long because apparently "The Nag" was done accompanying me on the long path to nowhere. I began to encounter a work situation with a co-worker that became quite conflictual. No matter what I did, it just got worse, never better. It finally came to a point that it was obvious that I needed to leave my beloved role as children's director. By then, I was *longing* to go to seminary. I was desperate to learn more about the Bible and to become a better leader.

My paltry bank account would pay for one quarter. I thought, "Well, at least I can get started." But, God had other ideas, and in one miraculous day, He provided all the funds I needed to complete the entire degree. He'd been telling me, "What I call forward, I provide for." He made good on that promise.

> *I wondered, "Where will I go?" I didn't have to wonder long because apparently "The Nag" was done accompanying me on the long path to nowhere.*

My four years of seminary training were some of the best in my life. I was a sponge seeking to soak up everything I could learn. I loved the atmosphere of challenge and sought to do my very best work. Perhaps, above all, I dreamed of the day when I would get my "call" and be invited "to play" with the other pastors—to have a respected position, to be listened to and included in important decisions, and to have the ability to speak into God's beloved kids' lives.

Interestingly, in my final months of seminary, the voice—which I now knew as the Holy Spirit—began to give me a vision for starting a new ministry that would equip all of God's people to know how they were gifted and called and to create pathways for that to happen. It seems the coveted pastor positions in churches weren't to be my call after all.

In those months of wrestling with the vision, I realized something: *I wanted to be someone who built a great big sandbox where everyone got to play!* Ministry needed to be something that everyone is invited into because we are all created with unique gifts and callings that need to be brought out in us, even if going to seminary wasn't in the cards.

Jesus got that. He didn't invite one scribe, Pharisee, Sadducee, or Levite to be one of His disciples. Instead, He invited everyday people—fishermen, tax collectors, and even zealots—to hang out and play. And, play they did. They had adventures beyond what they could have imagined.

They passed out a little boy's lunch to over 5,000 people, only to be busy packing up leftovers for take-home bags. They got to hold lots of healing sessions, one where Peter's mother-in-law was healed just in time to get up and make dinner for the party! Some of them got to meet Elijah and Moses on a mountain while they watched Jesus fill up with light and become transfigured. They also got to observe a herd of pigs run down a mountainside and plunge into the lake to drown.

The biggest time of play was when Jesus sent them out on their first missions trip. He put them together in pairs and gave them their marching orders: "Don't take anything for your journey—no credit cards, no change of clothes, no tents or sleeping bags. Just look for the people who will welcome you." Apparently, once they found those people, they were to fulfill their assignment to cast out demons, cure diseases, proclaim the Kingdom of God, and heal the sick (Luke 9:1-2).

I can only imagine a lot of shakin' going on inside them as they headed down the road, but once they got started, they discovered that they were experiencing the same power and authority that Jesus exercised when He was at play. They came back saying, *"Lord, even the demons obey us when we use your name"* (Luke 10:17).

I can only imagine the disciples thinking, "This is a whole lot more fun than sitting in synagogue memorizing and debating Torah." *Jesus knew how to make things come alive, and He invited others into it. When Jesus was around, it truly was a lot more like play than stiff religion.* He had a knack for finding the most interesting friends.

Take Zacchaeus. Jesus found him in a tree. His friend, Lazarus, had some interesting clothing choices; he was wearing the newest fashion called "grave clothes." Jesus wasn't' even afraid to include women. One of His favorite women friends was delivered from seven demons. He met another woman at a well in Samaria, which made her off limits in two ways. She was a woman and a Samaritan, which every good Jew knew was off limits. But Jesus and the Samaritan woman got along fabulously. His new friend invited Jesus and His disciples to stay for a two-day party. On and on it goes.

Jesus knew how to take faith outside where everyone got to play. The disciples learned it too. On the day of Pentecost, after Jesus' trip back to heaven, they experienced a massive windstorm that released tongues of fire on top of their heads, which they ran out to the Temple courtyard to display. Everyone was so impressed by them, Peter and the other disciples gained 3,000 new friends to invite onto the playground of life.

- When did we make faith so boring?
- Why did we develop big rules about how we should talk, pray, and behave?
- Why are we content to let faith be defined by a set of rules, rather than the One who teaches us to play?
- Why are we okay to let faith be about *believing* "the right thing," rather than *being in relationship* with the "right leader"?
- When did the "Christian box" become more important than the One who exists outside the box?

When I began to intentionally live out Kingdom, I realized that the separation between those who believe the "right things" and those who don't literally disappeared. Suddenly, I got to meet a lot more new friends. I found them in airports, in shopping malls, coffee shops, grocery store lines, traffic jams, public transportation, and stadiums. I got to hear their interesting stories and tell them mine.

I recently met a new friend named Vinnie. We met in the first two minutes of a line to get into a conference. Suddenly, we were talking about our mutual friend, Jesus, and being encouraged by one another's stories. He told me how Jesus had revealed to him how much He loved him. For 100 days, he saw one "sign" of it after another. Clouds would turn into hearts, at night he would get flooded with God's liquid love, and even his bathroom soap turned into a heart!

> *Jesus knew how to take faith outside*
> *where everyone got to play.*

The next day, I was with a group of people, and Vinnie told us more. Jesus had romanced him as His bride, and he was forever transformed by it. He mentioned he was a practicing homosexual when he met Jesus. He was so impacted by the depth of the Bridegroom's love for His bride, that he began sharing Jesus' overwhelming, loving pursuit with his friends. Over time, their identity as the Bride, deeply loved and inhabited by the Bridegroom, became their most important identity pursuit.

My mind went to all the discussions I've heard about whether homosexuals can "play" with other church goers. Do they get to belong as members? Do they get to go to seminary to learn the Bible? Can they be church leaders? Pastors? Denominational positions? But right in front of me, stood a handsome man who had been met and transformed by Jesus through the Bridegroom's love for His bride.

Then I knew once again what I've been learning over and over, that in the King's Kingdom, everyone gets to play!

REFLECT

- Does living your life of faith seem more like work or play? Why or why not?

DO SOMETHING

- Spend a week "playing" with Jesus. Ask Him to give you experiences that are very different than what you are used to living. Journal your experiences.

CHAPTER 10

THE MOVABLE TABERNACLE

When I was preparing to lead Missio Lux, I kept hearing the Lord say, "Think Tabernacle, not Temple." Hmmm, what did that mean exactly? So, I dug out my Old Testament and began to read up on the Tabernacle. Apparently, it was a mobile tent, easily taken down and transported from one location to another.

But it wasn't just any tent, it was the place of worship and sacrifice for the Israelites while they journeyed through the desert. It was carefully built. Moses received very specific instructions for how God wanted it formed. In fact, three times, God told Moses, "You must build this tabernacle and its furnishings exactly according to the pattern I will show you" (Exodus 25:9, 40; 26:30). The details for the Tabernacle were so intricate that the book of Exodus contains 12 chapters with detailed instructions for how to craft it.

So, where exactly did Moses get his instructions? Exodus 24 is one of my favorite chapters of the whole Bible because it is so unexpected. Here's the story. The Lord invited Moses and several of his friends—three priests and 70 of Israel's elders—to come up on the mountain to worship Him. After worshipping, Moses went down to the people and shared with them God's message. They responded, "We will do everything the Lord has commanded."

The next morning, Moses got up and built an altar at the foot of the mountain. Moses and some of the young Israelite men sacrificed some bulls as peace offerings. Then Moses took the Book of the Covenant and read it aloud to the people. Again, they responded, "We will do everything the Lord has commanded. We will obey."

Then Moses, the three priests, and 70 elders climbed up the mountain again. This is when it gets exciting. They saw the God of Israel! We are even given a description. "Under His feet there seemed to be a surface of brilliant blue lapis lazuli, as clear as the sky itself. And even though the nobles of Israel gazed upon God, He did not destroy them. In fact, they ate a covenant meal, eating and drinking in His presence" (Exodus 24:10-11).

It was after this extraordinary encounter with God that Moses stayed on the mountain for 40 days and nights. He met with God under the cloud of His glory and spent the time worshipping and receiving the instructions for how to build the Tabernacle. No wonder God was so insistent that His blueprint for the Tabernacle was followed to the letter. The Tabernacle was the place where He was planning to dwell.

It took a lot of people around nine months to complete the Tabernacle, but when it was done, the Lord told Moses to consecrate it on the first day of the Israelites' second year in the desert. Moses did the final preparations, and when he finished, the cloud of God's glory covered the Tabernacle and filled it (Exodus 40:34-35). In fact, God's glory was so strong, Moses couldn't even enter it.

Imagine it. An entire nation is living as nomads in the desert, but a tent is constructed and God's presence and glory comes and fills it so fully that all the people could do was worship from a distance. I often wonder what they were thinking as they experienced God's presence come around them.

It is here at the end of Exodus that I found out why the Lord kept pointing me back to the Tabernacle over the Temple. When the cloud lifted from the Tabernacle, the people knew they were to break camp and get ready to follow wherever the cloud mysteriously led them. The Tabernacle wasn't static and unmovable like the permanently built Temple. Instead it was flexible, easily taken up and down, giving the people the ability to respond to where and when God moved with His cloud and pillar of fire. God designed Missio Lux to be a group of people who weren't confined to a building or geographical location, but who were willing to follow Him wherever He directed us to move.

God was also highlighting all the miracles that took place during their journey. I think we often forget that it's not just the New Testament that is filled with signs and wonders; the Old Testament often reads like an action-packed movie. Exodus is certainly one of those books. Moses encounters the burning bush that speaks to him. Pharaoh and the Egyptians were the unlikely recipients of ten plagues that made their lives pretty miserable. The Red Sea dramatically parted, inviting the Israelites to cross over, and then became a watery tomb for the Egyptian army.

Once safely in the desert, the Israelites are reminded of God's presence through the glory cloud by day and the cloud of fire by night. The leaders were given an even greater gift through their invitation to the "banquet under an open heaven." Dream about what it must have been like to eat and drink under the brilliant throne of God, as they gazed upon His face.

Recently, I started reflecting on times of spiritual transitions, both in the Bible and in history. It's been fascinating to discover that a consistent pattern exists with an increase of signs and miracles in transitional seasons. Think about it. The Israelites were slaves for over 400 years, but the miracles started when Moses showed up to engage with Pharaoh for their freedom.

God was silent once again for 400 years between the time of the Old Testament and Jesus' earthly arrival. Then Zechariah, the father of John the Baptist, encountered Gabriel in the Holy of Holies, Joseph had dreams, and Mary had a heavenly visitation. Shepherds were surprised by an angelic light show in the sky, and a beautiful star guided wise men from distant lands to find and worship the baby King.

Signs and wonders always increase in times of transitional seasons.

Pentecost was another massive transition. Who would have guessed the fearful disciples would run to the Temple courtyard speaking in languages they'd never learned? Peter stood up and preached the sermon of his life, resulting in 3,000 new salvation births. Suddenly, miraculous signs and wonders became the disciples-turned-apostles' new normal. Healing a lame man on their way to the Temple was part of their supernaturally natural life. Even their shadows often left healing in their wake.

We are currently in another transitional season of history as we move from the Church Season to the Kingdom Age. Disorientation and confusion abounds causing many to wonder if God is even present anymore. Activities that used to satisfy and seem fruitful often fall flat. Morning worship services that brought peace and even new salvations often just seem boring. Pastoral leaders are frustrated, their congregations are restless, and even the latest conferences often seem ho hum as they recycle old ideas.

However, if we are willing to come up on the mountain to meet with God, as Moses did, we are often delighted with what He wants to show us. He parts the curtain between heaven and earth and shows us what He wants to give His kids. Surprises abound. Trips to the grocery store become opportunities for healing.

My good friend, Martha, and her son, Levi, were at the store when they heard God prompt them to pray for their checker who had a hip issue. Levi asked her if he could pray for her; it would only take 30 seconds, and she could keep her eyes open. She agreed and held out her hand for him to hold. He prayed a simple 30-second prayer, they paid for their food, and left.

> *Disorientation and confusion abounds when reclaiming faith and unboxing God.*

Weeks later, Martha was checking out, and the woman recognized her. She said, "Are you the woman whose son prayed for me? I have to tell you that my hip is all better. I know it was God, too, because I went to physical therapy for months and nothing happened. Right after the prayer, it stopped hurting!" Martha responded that God wanted her to know He loved her.

This is the Tabernacle in action!

We become the dwelling place for God's presence, and as we intentionally follow our King in His Kingdom ways, we discover that we can bring His presence into our everyday life. We become the ones who hear God whisper, "Your checker has a hip issue. I want her to know how much I love her, so will you pray for her?" We respond because we know we are loved, and when God mentions He wants to show up, all we need to do is take the step, and He does the rest. I find this life so much more fun and satisfying than sitting in church services *because I have a part to play.*

> *We become the dwelling place for God's presence, and as we intentionally follow our King in His Kingdom ways, we discover that we can bring His presence into our everyday life.*

Remember, in the Kingdom everyone gets to play. We don't need seminary degrees, church positions, or even a stamp of approval for a volunteer position. Instead, we need to know we are loved by the King, we are invited to partner with Him to seek first His Kingdom and establish it on earth, and we can trust that if He gives us an instruction, He will faithfully show up. After all, we are some of His favorite kids, but He has a long list of others He wants to include in His family!

I think another reason that the Lord continually redirected me to "think Tabernacle, not Temple" in those early days of forming Missio Lux is that it's a lot cheaper to build a tent than a temple. In fact, it's also a lot cheaper to run; since tents lack electricity and running water, the utility bills are non-existent! Seriously, remember our church budgeting conversations? After paying the mortgage and the utilities and, of course, the pastors' salaries, only 10% was left to divide up between all our ministries. Take away the building, and suddenly a whole lot of money is available to spend on actual needs that bring healing and freedom to our communities.

I am often quoted Hebrews 10:25, "Do not forsake meeting together," when people realize that we haven't joined an official church. But I often wonder if those quoting it remember that one of the biggest themes of Hebrews is the fulfillment of the heavenly Tabernacle. Perhaps they know this, but maybe forgot, that when Hebrews was written, the church consisted of small communities of people meeting in homes, moving in response to the cloud and fire over the tabernacles of God's presence within them. You may be one of the lucky ones who attends a church who remembers this. If so, you are blessed. But, if you discover or already know that your church's focus is only on the many wonderful opportunities *inside the building,* you may want to ask God if He has a bigger box in store for you, or possibly no box at all!

Maybe you are wondering how you can take steps to "live" Tabernacle, not Temple? Here's my recommendation: Do something outside of your ordinary.

- Pray before you run errands, asking your King to alert you if someone needs prayer and then be ready.
- Take a few Sunday mornings off from your church service, go to a park and just hang out. Observe what's happening and ask God to show you what He sees.
- Go to your child's school and walk around it as you pray for the administration, teachers, students, and families.
- Contact your governmental leaders and tell them you are praying for them (and actually do it!).
- Pray a prayer of blessing over fathers spending time with their children.
- Invite your Muslim co-worker to share lunch together as you build a friendship.
- Offer to help unload groceries for the single mother across the street in your neighborhood.
- Use your imagination to dream about what a reclaimed faith with no box around God would look like to you, and then go and live it!

Each time you take one small step, you are walking intentionally with your King in partnering to establish His Kingdom, as the Tabernacle, following the cloud of His glory as heaven connects to earth.

Oh, and one more thing, where would you rather be? The Israelites in the desert told Moses, "We will obey," even as they begged Moses to cover his face from God's glory that was emanating through it. They had no appreciation or desire for the glory. They chose to stay at the bottom of the mountain out of fear. The statement, "We will obey," indicates the Israelites didn't really know the heart of their heavenly Father who is far more interested in our worship that leads to a heart to want to "know" God and to listen to His voice. Moses and Joshua spent time worshipping in the tent of meeting, and even after Moses left, Joshua remained.

I, for one, plan to live my life as a Joshua in the Tabernacle worshipping Jesus the King.

REFLECT

- If you actually followed a cloud or pillar of fire, where do you believe it would take you? Spend some time envisioning what would happen as a result.

DO SOMETHING

- Believe that you have a guiding cloud and pillar of fire. Give God permission to guide you. Enjoy the ride!

CHAPTER 11

WE GET THE FRUIT OF OUR FOCUS

One of my favorite statements is "You get the fruit of your focus." If we focus on disappointment, we will most invariably be disappointed by life. If we focus on exercise, we will get a healthier, stronger body. If we focus on stress, we will feel stressed. If we focus on relationships, we will most likely have connected, meaningful friendships.

The same reality goes for where we put our focus in our spiritual life. Colossians 3:1 states, *"Since you have been raised to new life with Christ, set your sights on the realities of heaven, where Christ sits at God's right hand in the place of honor and power."* Paul then tells us in verse two to think about the things of heaven, not the things of earth.

Did you realize that our brain acts like a guard to protect the rest of our body? If something tries to come into our lives that our brain doesn't recognize, it actually kicks it out. Here's an example. If someone tells us we look beautiful, but if we've thought we were overweight and unattractive for our whole lives, our brain won't receive it. We will continue to believe the old lie. In the same way, if we believe that we don't deserve to have a fulfilling life, when we start to receive blessings from our heavenly Father, we may disregard them, excuse them away, or even sabotage them.

I've long considered that God isn't all that interested in what we do. He's mostly interested in what we believe or think because our thoughts and beliefs influence how connected we stay in relationship with Him.

When we believe God loves us and is working to bring about our good, it often leads us to fruitful habits in life, rather than sinful ones, because we make choices out of our love for God, rather than fear of punishment for something we might do.

> *God isn't all that interested in what we do. He's mostly interested in what we believe or think because our thoughts and beliefs influence how connected we stay in relationship with Him.*

This was a very new thought in Jesus' day. We see this in the story of a curious crowd who tracked Him down after He had walked on the water to find the disciples in the midst of a huge storm. He got into the boat, and suddenly, they were on the other side of the lake (John 6:22-29). After the crowd found Him there, they wanted to know how He got there. Jesus refused to answer their question but instead encouraged them to spend their energies seeking the eternal life He offered. It was for this His Father gave His seal of approval.

The crowd's key question became, "We want to perform God's works, too. What should we *do*?" Jesus answered with this provocative statement, "This is the only work God wants from you: *believe in the one he has sent.*"

Do you see it? We often want to "do" the right things to please God, but what actually makes His heart skip with joy is when we *believe* He is a good Father who wants the best for us. This is the foundation for walking out a relationship of trust with Him. When this becomes our overarching focus, suddenly good things begin to happen to us, or maybe we begin to recognize them for the first time!

The summer we moved to California and I was on the sabbatical from Missio Lux, I was in a lot of pain. I felt disoriented and disappointed because I saw what I thought was my destiny slipping away. I was outside stretching one morning, and I cried out, "God, what am I going to do?"

He answered, "Enjoy My good gifts today." I was asking the big "future" question, but He answered me with a "now" statement. He went on to say, "Tamara, look up. What do you see?"

I said, "The sun."

I felt Him smile and say, "Exactly." (We'd moved from Seattle where the sun was a lot more elusive.) Then, He said, "What's in your garden?"

I answered, "Fruit trees laden with fruit, roses everywhere in full bloom."

He asked me, "Did you plant those?"

No, I didn't. He asked me to look at the swimming pool and asked me if I was happy about the pool. I smiled at this point because I began to realize He'd surrounded me with a paradise. I was letting my disorientation from the move and my disappointment about the status of Missio Lux suck all my energies into despair, rather than reveling in the beauty and good gifts all around me.

That conversation continued for the entire summer. Each day, I would ask God the question, "What do You want me to do?" His answer would be the same, "Enjoy My good gifts today." And good gifts came in abundance!

Bill and I flew internationally, and we got upgraded to first class status. We went to a winery party, and we were escorted to the VIP section for no other reason than I guess we were VIPs to God! Our youngest daughter decided to move from Chicago to Santa Rosa and brought an adorable little puppy. (I LOVE dogs...and my daughter, of course!) Each day brought a new surprise!

That summer changed me. I went from a mindset that God was pleased with me when I worked hard in ministry to a realization that He was a loving father who wanted to please His daughter by lavishing her with good gifts, even when I felt like I was in the middle of a massive failure. I began a slow knowing that it isn't what we *do* that creates fruit, but it's what we *align with*...because we get *the fruit of our focus.*

I can now say this: Believing that God is a generous, good Father who loves to fulfill His kids' hearts' desires has led me into a far more satisfying and fun life. This next story illustrates more what my life looks like now.

I was in Phoenix leading a "Reclaim Identity" workshop. When it was finished, I was flying to Denver to await my oldest daughter's arrival from England for her bridal shower. I had never flown Southwest, so I never even thought to check in that morning for my late afternoon flight. When I got to the gate, they told me the flight was full, but to sit down, and if there was a seat left over, they would let me on. I sat down, feeling relaxed, because I didn't have a time pressure to get to Denver.

> *I began a slow knowing that it isn't what we do that creates fruit, but it's what we align with...because we get the fruit of our focus.*

After just a few minutes, they called my name. I expected to find my seat in the middle of the back row, but as I entered the plane, I saw a seat in the front row. Southwest has open seating, so I asked the two people sitting there if that seat was taken. They answered no, that many people almost sat there, but then suddenly passed it by. I said, "Well, I'll take it" and sat down.

I started to chat with them, and the woman on my right told me that she was a student at Denver Seminary, the same school I had attended. I asked her if they were still doing the training and mentoring program, as it was the most impactful during my time at the seminary. She said yes and that she'd been praying all weekend for God to give her a mentor. She'd gone down several paths, but no one had been available to commit.

I said, "I'll be your mentor. I have a passion to encourage women in ministry."

She answered, "Well, I have a list for who I am looking for. I want her to be a published author, speak and lead retreats, and know about healing prayer."

I smiled and said, "That's what I do. I write, speak, and lead retreats, and oh, by the way, I started a healing ministry in Seattle," as I passed her my book, *Identity Crisis: Reclaim the True You.* She looked at me absolutely stunned.

The rest of the flight, my new friend, Martha, kept saying, "I can't believe this."

I said, "This is what good fathers do. They go out of their way to please their kids."

I love to tell this story because it illustrates just how far God will go to answer our prayers. He orchestrated a meeting on an airplane in a city where neither of us lived, just so Martha could have the mentor of her dreams(!) and begin the journey of realizing just how good her heavenly Father was.

My four years in Santa Rosa changed me. I was used to being in the center of things in Seattle, but when we moved to Santa Rosa, we were hours away from San Francisco and Sacramento or the East Bay, so it was a big commitment to travel to those areas to meet the "important" people of my denomination or other ministries. I knew that I was to stay put and to keep writing, to build Reclaim (see books listed at the end of this book), and to lead Reclaim Identity retreats.

In my hiddenness, the Lord began to teach me Kingdom strategies that were simple to implement but created a ripple-like impact. He opened up the Old Testament to me by showing me that it was a training manual in the natural (earthly) realm for how we are to navigate in the supernatural Kingdom realm.

> *God taught me that my voice*
> *has influence in heaven.*

But, most of all, He taught me that my voice has influence in heaven. He began to teach me the countercultural reality that when I prayed, heaven listened and responded. I began to understand that even if I couldn't see the outcome and may never know what took place as I prayed, one day, I would see the harvest in heaven.

One of my favorite passages to pray was Ezekiel 37 where God took his friend, Ezekiel, to a valley of dry bones and asked him what he saw. He answered, "You know Lord." But, the Lord didn't want that religious answer, so He asked him again. This time Ezekiel answered, "I see a valley of dry bones." Then the Lord smiled and said, "Exactly, here's what I want you to say."

As Ezekiel spoke out the message God had for him, the dry bones began to shake. Then they became skeletons that came to life, and eventually, God brought the whole army—who is Israel in the natural realm but represents all of God's beloved kids in the supernatural realm—home to their own land, the place of their true destiny!

I loved the simplicity of that exchange. I don't have to figure it out; I just need to be in relationship with God and learn to hear His voice like Ezekiel did. I speak it out, and He does the rest. Wow! That's a lot different than what I learned to do in ministry.

Here's the catch, however. I can't measure it on earth. I can't brag about it to my friends on Facebook. I can't build a ministry on it or take a paycheck from it. I've had to change my mind from focusing on the things on earth to setting my sights on the realities of heaven. It's like learning a new skill, riding a bike, or driving a car. It feels hard and uncomfortable at first, but as I've learned the rhythm, it feels light and easy, like Jesus described in Matthew 11:28-30:

> *Then Jesus said, "Come to me, all of you who are weary and carry heavy burdens, and I will give you rest. Take my yoke upon you. Let me teach you, because I am humble and gentle, and you will find rest for your souls. For my yoke fits perfectly, and the burden I give you is light."*

I love this invitation even more in *The Message:*

> *Are you tired? Worn out? Burned out on religion? Come to me. Get away with me and you'll recover your life. I'll show you how to take a real rest. Walk with me and work with me—watch how I do it. Learn the unforced rhythms of grace. I won't lay anything heavy or ill-fitting on you. Keep company with me and you'll learn to live freely and lightly.*

This is our invitation for this season of transition between the Church Season and the Kingdom Age. For all of us who believed that working hard was the way to please God, I invite you to spend 90 days focusing on this profound invitation Jesus gave us. It will change your focus, and suddenly, you will see fruit trees laden with harvest all around you. Choose your favorite fruit and sit down to enjoy its juice dripping down your chin as you savor the gift of partnership with your loving King.

REFLECT

- Make a list of all the ways you "serve" God. On the opposite column, make a list of the good gifts you would like God to give you. Dream big! No dream is too small or absolutely too big!

DO SOMETHING

- Spend 90 days focusing on Jesus' invitation in Matthew 11. Repeat this out loud to yourself at least once a day. What is He saying about what you are doing?

  _____ (your name), are you tired? Worn out? Burned out on religion? Come to me. Get away with me and you'll recover your life. I'll show you how to take a real rest. Walk with me and work with me—watch how I do it. Learn the unforced rhythms of grace. I won't lay anything heavy or ill-fitting on you. Keep company with me and you'll learn to live freely and lightly._

CHAPTER 12

JESUS AS KING

I still remember the day when Jesus invited me to know Him in a different way, beyond loving *Savior,* who saved me from my sin, and beyond *Lord,* who has taught me how to live with Him as the center and foundation of my life. This day, the challenge was to know Him as the *Resurrected King of the Universe* to whom every knee in heaven, earth, and under the earth must bow.

It was Advent (remember, I love Advent), and we were singing Christmas carols at church. I love those carols, and that day, they brought back so many happy childhood memories of singing and lighting candles in our newly planted church. I belonged, I was loved, and all seemed right with the world!

As we were singing, my heart bursting with joy, I sensed Jesus say, "Why is everyone so happy to acknowledge Me as the baby in the manger? When will they discover the baby in the manger was sent to earth to become the ruling King of the Universe? Tamara, are you willing to let Me lead you into this reality?" Never one to back down from a challenge, especially from Jesus, I said, "Of course, I'd love to come on this journey with You."

That invitation has been life changing for me. I've thought about why it is so easy to ignore Jesus' kingly identity. When we read the Gospels, we see a man who was gentle with the poor and disenfranchised. We observe

Jesus giving away power and modeling sacrifice at every turn. I think it is easy to unconsciously equate His humility as weakness.

After all, when He entered Jerusalem, He didn't come on a majestic horse. He rode an unbroken donkey. When the soldiers came for Jesus in the Garden of Gethsemane, He didn't resist arrest; in fact, He told His disciples to put their weapons away. He allowed Himself to be led into a mock trial, stayed silent against His accusers, and the only question He answered with any detail was about His role as king.

> *"Why is everyone so happy to acknowledge Me as the baby in the manger? When will they discover the baby in the manger was sent to earth to become the ruling King of the Universe?*

To be fair, we are given a whole lot more detail about Jesus' life on earth than we are about His kingly reign in heaven. When we listen to sermons or teachings, we most often hear about how Jesus walked on earth. This is important, but when this is the only aspect of Jesus that is explored, it's actually easy to forget that His purpose was to come to reclaim the universe, and *He invites us to partner with Him to do it.*

This was part of Jesus' process with me. He invited me to know Him as King, so that I could respond to His next invitation: *Would I sit next to Him on the throne?*

I think I responded with something like, "Okay, Lord, I will think about it. This feels like a responsibility that seems bigger than me."

At that point, He smiled and said, "It is. That's why you need to know Me as King."

So, I began to take tentative steps. I started searching the New Testament for direction on accepting the King's invitation. I found a passage that I especially loved because it starts around the table.

Look! Here I stand at the door and knock. If you hear my voice and open the door, I will come in, and we will share a meal as friends. Those who are victorious will sit with me on my throne, just as I was victorious and sat with my Father on his throne (Revelation 3:20-21).

I was taught in Sunday School that verse 20 was a salvation passage, but it describes more than salvation and our life in heaven. It is about the intimacy that takes place when we share a place at the table with King Jesus. He is inviting us to go beyond our identity as "well done, good and perfect *servant.*" He is acknowledging us as His *friend.* Now, that's something I can embrace with a great big YES!

But the relationship doesn't stop at the table; it leads us to the throne room. And when we look up at the throne, we see it is big enough for two. But many of us can't accept this and create an escape route from it. When we read that His throne is reserved for those who are victorious, we respond with, "Don't You see all the ways I've screwed up?" No! God doesn't see those screw ups because Jesus covered those in His crucifixion. It is victory that paves the way for our walk on the red carpet toward the throne, where He sits with great anticipation for our new partnership to start.

So, I said yes to King Jesus. I walked the red carpet. I accepted the scepter and allowed myself to be escorted onto the throne. But now what? He turned and looked at me and said He had a gift for me. He handed me a great big key ring filled with keys.

Oh, I thought, "I get it. This is the same key ring You gave to Peter when You commissioned him to lead Your church, to be the small rock under the shadow of the big rock" (Matthew 16:16-19). So, I said thank you as I accepted King Jesus' gift. But, then I wasn't sure what to do with them, so I asked Him how to use my new keys.

"It's simple. Faith is the key. The key opens the lock when you declare My heavenly purposes."

"Well, King Jesus, how am I to know what those are?"

He responded again, "It's easy. I will tell you what to say."

Then I remembered Ezekiel 37 and the valley of the dry bones that

I described in the last chapter. The Lord told Ezekiel, *"Speak a prophetic message to these bones and say, 'Dry bones, listen to the word of the LORD!...the Sovereign LORD says: Look! I am going to put breath into you and make you live again! I will put flesh and muscles on you and cover you with skin. I will breath into you, and you will come to life. Then you will know that I am the LORD'"* (Ezekiel 37:4-6).

Ezekiel followed the Lord's instructions, and the valley of dry bones became a living, breathing army. That must have been a spectacular sight. I have to guess Ezekiel probably didn't have anything more exciting than this take place in his life as a prophet.

Here's the good news as I see it. King Jesus is inviting us to take the words in Ezekiel off the page. In other words, He wants us to be like Ezekiel. As we begin to practice speaking and declaring God's words, we will also see the valley of dry bones *in our lives* coming to life.

The King's heavenly resources are all there: an invitation to the table for connecting deeply as intimate friends, His invitation to sit on the throne, and the heavenly key ring in our hands, as our ears hear King Jesus' directives and our mouths declare them.

Interestingly, we discover the Bible does give us a clue about the transition from the Church Season to the Kingdom Age. Revelation 2-3 speaks to the seven churches, but the fourth chapter launches a different theme with an invitation. John tells us as he looked, he saw a door standing open in heaven, and a voice said, *"Come up here, and I will show you what must happen after this"* (Revelation 4:1).

So, what did he see? A throne room with a king sitting on it. John had the massive privilege to see heaven in action, as millions and millions of angels worshipped the King, and 24 elders laid their crowns at His feet. They all sang out,

> *You are worthy to take the scroll and break its seals and open it. For you were killed, and your blood has ransomed people for God from every tribe and language and people and nation. And you have caused them to become God's kingdom and his priests. And they will reign on the earth (Revelation 5:9-10).*

It seems the transition from the Church Season to the Kingdom Age involves the Body of Christ receiving the invitation from the King of the Universe to become trained priests in His Kingdom, reigning on the earth. I have to say at this point, accepting this invitation is a lot different than volunteering to serve at church ushering, taking care of babies, teaching Sunday School, and setting up chairs for an event.

I was further blown away as King Jesus led me to Daniel 7. Once again, we find another prophet, Daniel, being ushered into the throne room. He saw someone like the Son of Man coming in the clouds. He was given authority, honor, and sovereignty over the entire world, so that all people would obey Him. His rule is eternal; and His Kingdom will never be destroyed (Daniel 7:13-14).

> *In the Kingdom Age, we are invited by the King of the Universe to be trained to become a Kingdom of Priests who reign on the earth.*

That sounds a lot like what John observed in Revelation. But, as I continued, I was astounded to read: *"But in the end, the holy people of the Most High will be given the kingdom, and they will rule forever and ever"* (Daniel 7:18). I discovered that Daniel 7 states—not just once, not even twice, but three times—that God's people will reign over kingdoms in heaven.

As I sat with Daniel 7 for some time, I suddenly understood that the reason we are being trained to become a kingdom of priests on earth is to prepare us for our assignment in heaven—to reign in the kingdom! When you think about eternity and heaven, we realize our training on earth is a fraction of the time we will spend in heaven. The end game was now clear. It's vital for us to say yes to King Jesus' invitation to join His training team, so that we are ready for our heavenly position as royal heirs, partnering with our True Sovereign, Jesus Christ, King of the Universe.

I want to end this chapter with a sense of my excitement to be alive in this specific point of history. The adventure is here, and our opportunities are endless. God has truly given us permission, and even a sense of urgency, to "unbox" Him!

Remember when I warned you there is a point of no return? You have a choice.

- Which way will you go?

- Will you choose the road of adventure into the unfamiliar?

- Or, will you choose to play it safe and stay within the comfort of the world that you know and understand?

If you choose the safe confines of your comfort zone, be careful, because it's going to be shaken. The faith world you know and understand is quickly transitioning into the Kingdom world which awaits us, so we may know and follow our King.

REFLECT

- Consider the cost of saying "yes." What will you give up? What will you receive?

- Spend time reflecting on whether you feel satisfied with your life of faith. If you have even the smallest "no" in your heart, take the plunge and say "yes" to King Jesus, and go wherever He takes you.

DO SOMETHING

- Read Luke 4 and discover the different stages of identity training Jesus went through after His baptism at the end of Luke 3.

- Consider purchasing 5 Stages of Identity: Success Reclaimed for your next read. (Go to ReclaimInitiative.com).

CHAPTER 13

INVISIBILITY CAN CHANGE THE WORLD

Why do you think Jesus often told people to stay quiet after He performed a miracle? I think I understand why He told the leper not to broadcast his healing (Matthew 8:1-4). When Jesus touched him, that made Him become socially unclean like the leper. But, in Matthew 9:27-30, two blind men called out to Jesus for healing. Jesus asked the key question, *"Do you believe I can make you see?"* When they replied, "Yes!" Jesus touched their eyes, and suddenly they could see. Imagine their excitement, but Jesus' follow-up instructions included, *"Don't tell anyone about this."* In fact, Matthew tells us Jesus was stern with them. Why?

> Don't miracles give glory to God?
> Don't miracles help people recognize Jesus' true identity?
> Don't miracles help to build momentum for a ministry?
> Don't miracles help to add fuel to a revolution?

Why would Jesus go out of His way to stay hidden, especially when He only had three years to accomplish His mission? Remember when His brothers taunted Him about going up to the festival so others could find out about Him? Jesus went, but only in hiddenness (John 7:10). It seems Jesus had a different priority.

He gives us a clue when His opening statement is *"The Kingdom of God is near"* (Mark 1:15). He told stories about the Kingdom, and they almost always revolved around hiddenness: the yeast in the dough (Matthew 13:33), the treasure in the field (Matthew 13:44), the smallest seed in the ground (Mark 4:30-32). Even the parable of the banquet called for guests to be found in the *hidden* byways and highways (Luke 14:16-24).

I spent three years in Santa Rosa building Reclaim Initiative. I called a team together, wrote retreat curriculums, and started hosting and leading retreats for those who were hungry to reclaim their identity. I had a growing blog list, prayer list, contacts for retreat invitations, and announcements for the many new books I was publishing (see www.ReclaimInitiative.com or at the back of this book). I was building a platform because I believed, along with many others, that I had valuable things to say.

But, one day, after Jesus and I experienced an especially sweet time of worship, my King gave me a new instruction. He told me how proud He was of my work with the Reclaim Identity retreats and all that I had done to create and build the foundation of Reclaim. Then He asked me to take the ministry *underground*!

Really? After three years of faithfully developing a ministry, so others could know freedom in their identities, lives, and destinies? But, in my spirit, I knew His voice, and I knew that He must have a reason for His request. So, I went quiet. I stopped blogging, writing books, sending out invites to the retreats, and even pruned my prayer list to a few.

A few years earlier, I would have chafed under such an instruction. I would have wrestled and complained and argued. I probably would have even felt like a victim, believing God was against me. But, after three years of intense Kingdom training, I understood what He was asking me. I knew that harvest comes from the Kingdom seeds in the ground that are left there to grow. I also knew that if I was going to be in His timing, I needed to move out of my current fruit-bearing season and transition into an abiding season (John 15).

I lived in Sonoma County at the time. If you haven't been there, go and revel in the abundant vineyards all around. I loved to watch their seasons. We moved there in January, so the grape vines were stark, just sticks in the ground standing out naked. But, in early spring, I could see the tiny buds blooming, and by summer, the vines were in all their glory with lavish green leaves and large clumps of juicy grapes hanging from the vines. Autumn was one of my favorite times because the leaves would turn a multitude of colors, and when the sun hit them just right, I actually felt like I was in heaven. It was a feast for my eyes. Though I enjoyed their beauty, I knew that winter was coming in just a few weeks, and the vines would change as the leaves began to drop onto the ground.

Our times with Jesus are meant to be the same. We have buds of new birth that blossom into full harvest, and it is glorious, but eventually, the leaves begin to drop, and winter is imminent. If we try to ignore winter and find grapes to harvest, we will be sorely disappointed. It is in that time of silence, of massive pruning, of starkness, that we find life again. When we acknowledge it for what it is—a time to go into rest and communion with our King—we gain the benefit, and we are fertilized for our next fruitful season.

I didn't realize when Jesus asked me to "go underground" that He was preparing to use my abiding season to make a big move. Within weeks, He had birthed a miracle with a surprise relocation to Denver! When people ask us why we moved, we can't really say, except that God moved heaven and earth to move not just my husband and I, but also our two daughters and a son-in-law!

> **It is in that time of silence, of massive pruning, of starkness, that we find life again.**

It's been such a gift but moving across country is a *lot* of work. I will forever cherish those weeks of time with King Jesus, when He poured into me, preparing me for a very new season of life. I thought that when I came to Denver, I would be freed from His request to stay underground and could become known again. I was really happy when a big opportunity came my way. A major Christian radio station wanted to record my daily advent readings from my book, *Seeking the Christmas Lamb*. This would most definitely put Reclaim Initiative on the map, and people would find their way to all the other resources that I'd developed.

I was visiting my daughter in New York City at the end of October, and the last day I was there, I was awakened early by Jesus. I knew it was Him, but there was a lot of spiritual static, and I was having a hard time identifying His voice. Eventually, as I pressed in to hear, I found Him above the fray.

He gave me a choice. He said that I could choose one but not both. He told me that I could go the external route and partner with the radio station for Advent, and I would see a "measure of fruit," or I could go the way of the internal, stay underground, and serve my family (our daughter and son in law were living with us temporarily). If I did, there would be a big eternal harvest.

> **So, in the midst of our frantic search for meaning, for recognition, for our lives to matter, it's right in front of us: We can literally change the world...if we are willing to be invisible.**

Once again, a few years ago, I would have chosen the radio station because I believed being known on earth was what it was all about. But, after my years of Kingdom training and the relationship I'd developed with the King, I knew that I wanted His choice. I wanted the fruit that would last for all eternity. So, I laid down the radio opportunity. I stayed quiet and continued to serve my family.

What I didn't know would happen is that my husband would receive a stage three cancer diagnosis on the second day of Advent. He ended up having a six-hour surgery to remove his kidney on December 20th. The entire season of Advent became filled with doctor appointments, medical tests, phone calls to doctors, anxious waiting, and a five-day hospital stay. If you do the math, you'll see he came home on Christmas Day.

It wasn't the Advent I had envisioned, but there was a supernatural grace surrounding us that made that season actually joyful. Everywhere we looked, the King and His Kingdom were present. I will always cherish our season of death becoming resurrection.

Though my story ends well with Bill getting a clean bill of health, the challenge to stay invisible has been an ongoing one. A passage in the Sermon on the Mount has helped me stay centered. Sandwiched in the middle of the Sermon on the Mount is this statement: "You can enter God's Kingdom only through the narrow gate. The highway to destruction is broad, and its gate is wide for the many who choose that way. But the gateway to life is very narrow and the road is difficult, and only a few ever find it" (Matthew 7:13-14).

This seems like a dichotomy to me when I now understand that in the Kingdom, everyone gets to play! But, when we are truly honest with ourselves, Jesus modeled and taught some leadership lessons that are a bit hard to swallow:

- He chose humility over power positions.
- He taught us to sacrifice rather than to be served.
- He demonstrated compassion rather than control.
- He called us to servanthood over authoritarian leadership.
- He chose heavenly authority rather than earthly authority.
- He elevated hiddenness over popularity.

Even as I write this, I know how far I am from living as Jesus lived. Still, I sometimes find myself chafing at my hidden position, frustrated that the Body of Christ doesn't see the sacrifice I am making for them. It feels good to be known, to be seen, to be relevant, to be retweeted, to be followed, to be liked. Sometimes I experience disrespect from others in ministry because they don't think I am doing anything important. I sometimes want to cry out, "I am plowing new ground in the vineyard, so you can pick the fruit."

But, after I come back to my center, I realize, once again, that following the way of the King in His Kingdom brings me right into the place of His heart and invitation: "I came that you might have an abundant life which fulfills all your deepest heart's desires" (John 10:10). So, in the midst of our frantic search for meaning, for recognition, for our lives to matter, it's right in front of us: We can literally change the world...*if we are willing to be invisible.*

Follow the way of the King, who gave up His life with His arms outstretched in invitation to those who were willing to look up and into His face of love, His invitation to life, and rebirth into His heavenly Kingdom. When He declared, "It is finished," He was thinking of you. He prepared the pathway into the narrow gate, and He offers His hand in invitation to walk with you through it.

How will you respond to His outstretched hand?

REFLECT

- Reflect on a time when you have done something that no one knew about, but it ended up bringing forth good. How did it feel? What did it bring up in you?

- Take some time to consider how your hidden seeds may be bringing forth a harvest.

DO SOMETHING

- Commit to doing acts of kindness in secret for the next seven days. Don't tell anyone about them.

- Take some time to journal what God may do with your hidden seeds of faith in action.

CHAPTER 14

WHICH WAY WILL YOU GO?

O ne Sunday, we were invited to attend an "official" church service
for the first time in a very long time. As we drove into the city and
parked, it was nice to see young families walking to the service, children in
tow. We walked into the building, observing an old church that was being
given a facelift with some creative paint, decorations, and burning candles.

My husband and I got our drink of choice and sat down in the spacious
pew, while the worship band began to play. They obviously had some
talent, as the musicians were skilled at their instruments, and the singers
not only had beautiful tone, but also passion in their voices.

When the time came for the sermon, I was delighted to see a woman
stand up to preach. She was interesting to listen to and drew the audience
in with some funny points that made us all laugh. Her sermon was followed
by communion, intinction style (when the bread is dipped into the cup),
where we all lined up and received Christ's body and blood through
two servers. When everyone was served, we sang two more songs, did a
community benediction, and the service was finished.

As my husband and I drove away, we reflected on the service. We had
a very pleasant experience. We were comfortable sitting in the pew with
our friends, as our coffee warmed our hands. We enjoyed the worship and
the sermon. But, as we dug deeper, I realized that, once again, we'd heard
just a few sentences of Scripture read off an iPad through the service. I

had to dig to remember the challenge we received to live more like Jesus. I thought about whether I'd connected with God during the experience.

Although I could sense the Spirit's presence throughout the worship, I realized we'd been given no time to sit still and to listen to God's voice in the service. We'd never been told to expect to hear God speak to us. Just by the nature of our stance, *sitting* in the pews, and the leader's presence on the stage several feet *above* us, it communicated to us that they were the ones who heard God, and we were to listen to them, so we could hear from Him too.

I also remembered that I had read about the small groups they offered. As I scanned the list (strategically positioned in the bathroom), I realized I didn't see one choice that would help equip the congregation to go deeper in studying and understanding the Bible, in hearing God speak, or in following King Jesus to seek first His kingdom.

As I reflected on that church experience, I thought of the difference between what is good and what is best. I like to ask people the name for the tree in the Garden of Eden that Adam and Eve were forbidden to eat from, and most often, the answer is the tree of the knowledge of evil. What many easily forget is that it was called the tree of the knowledge of *good* and evil. I've come to realize that *good* truly is the enemy of God's *best*. The reason, of course, is that while we are busy enjoying the *good*, we are rarely motivated to *pursue the best pathway.*

> ### I've come to realize that good truly is the enemy of God's best.

Jesus tells us the best is God's Kingdom path, and He also reminds us that eating from the best often means encountering resistance. This reality brings us back to the choice between the broad road and the narrow path. He empathically states, *"The gateway to life is very narrow and the road is difficult, and only a few ever find it"* (Matthew 7:14).

Very recently, I was home alone on a Monday night. At 9:30 p.m., I heard four very loud knocks on our front door. I went uneasily to open the door, wondering who would brave the stormy weather to visit unannounced. I looked out the window and my concern grew, for I couldn't see a car in our driveway. I wondered aloud who would walk to our house, which is rather remote, up our very steep driveway. My dogs and I slowly opened the door and said, "Hello?" No one. No answer. I got the flashlight and shone it all around, being grateful that at least I knew I didn't make it up because my dogs continued to bark with anticipation to greet the mysterious visitor.

I quickly sent out several "Help me" prayers by text, as I felt fear roll through me. After several minutes, I got two texts back saying, "I've been praying, and I sense it was the Lord." I then realized that while I waited, I was hearing the Scripture, *"Behold, I stand at the door and knock"* (Revelation 3:20, NKJV). With that, I became peaceful and went to bed without giving it another thought.

The next morning, curiosity took hold of me, so I asked the Lord, "If it was You, why? What were You saying?" What came to me was a great sense of urgency. "It's time for My beloved people to wake up and open the door for Me to come in and share a meal with them, as we prepare for us to partner together for the expansion of My Kingdom!"

May I be the knock on your door as I ask you, "Where may He be calling you to wake up and answer the door?"

> Could it be to the reality that you are God's beloved child and your true home is in heaven?
>
> Could it be embracing the fact that the Kingdom is within you because God lives in you?
>
> Could it be joining with other Kingdom seekers in shared relationship, feasting around the table and experiencing life with the King?
>
> Could it be discovering that the very One who created you actually speaks to you, as He—Immanuel, God with us—joins you in your sorrows and revels in your joy?

Could it be experiencing the rest for your soul (and body) that Jesus invited you to experience, as you walk with Him because His yoke is easy and His burden light?

Could it be discovering your true divine design and living God's unique and fulfilling destiny for your life?

Could it be experiencing the upside-down Kingdom priority system where one simple act can have transformational impact?

Could it be joining with people who are different than you and finding common language and experience, broadening your worldview and building bridges of friendship with those, just perhaps, your church or denomination were unintentionally (or not) keeping out?

Could it be caring for the poor, praying for the suffering saints around the world, or actively engaging in fighting for justice for those who are living in unjust situations?

Could it be the way of following the King and His Kingdom ways, recognizing the great adventure He invites us into as He hands you your very own heavenly key ring?

Could it be reclaiming your faith in the midst of this turbulent season of history that is quickly becoming post-church?

I want to conclude with one more story. We were in Edinburgh a few years ago, touring as a family. When we got to the cathedral where John Knox preached, they stated that it was off limits to tourists because they were ready to start their worship service. Bill and I looked at one another and decided we'd like to join in as participants in the worship. As my eyes feasted on the beautiful cathedral, and my ears listened—captivated by the mysterious, unseen singing monks—I asked King Jesus a simple question, "Where are You?"

I sensed He wanted to answer that question, but nothing emerged during the service. At the conclusion of the sermon, we were invited to come to the entrance of the church for a child's baptism. As I stood facing the door, I had a vivid picture of Jesus opening the door, looking straight at me, and then walking out as the door slammed shut behind Him. I think I gasped out loud at that point, as I felt a very real pang go through my heart.

> *I grieved for months following that experience, but I finally had to come to the realization that if Jesus left the building, He was calling me to follow.*

I grieved for months following that experience, but I finally had to come to the realization that if Jesus left the building, He was calling me to follow. My heart told me that if Jesus has left the building to pursue His Kingdom, I don't want to be anywhere He is not.

If you've made it this far in the book, could King Jesus also be beckoning you to follow Him into the unknown adventure of His Kingdom? Let me encourage you. Wrestle. Process. Journal. Read. Pray. Fast. Listen. Meditate. But, eventually answer God's key question: *Which way will you go?* As you make your decision, consider what you may be giving up to continue in your status quo.

- Will you be continuing to live in a season that is quickly becoming "the past," as our culture becomes more and more post-church?

- Will you miss the opportunity to discover many of God's beloved kids who need to know God cares about them and loves them too?

- Will you miss discovering and living out your true destiny?

- Most of all, will you miss the adventurous journey Jesus is inviting you to experience as you allow God to "unbox Himself"?

Of course, continuing the status quo has its definite advantages. You won't upset the apple cart with your family and friends if you continue to do what's always been comfortable and pleasant. If you are a professional Christian (meaning if you get paid for what you do in the church or Christian organizations), your paycheck will remain secure (at least for a little bit longer). If you are a Christian leader, you won't have to explain your decision and experience the misunderstanding and, often, rejection, which invariably comes with a shift in behavior and rhythms of life. *You won't have to risk getting kicked out of the church by someone other than God.*

> ### *Could King Jesus also be beckoning you to follow Him into the unknown adventure of His Kingdom?*

If you feel that you lack the courage to take this step, remember Peter. He was a bold disciple within the confines of his faith as he knew it. When it seemed that Jesus was imploding through His arrest, Peter became a very scared follower. He denied knowing Jesus to three servants, people of absolutely no earthly importance. But, after he experienced the power of Pentecost through the Holy Spirit becoming sealed within him, Peter, *the fearful disciple,* became a *fearless apostle.* Even though he was arrested and brought before the Jewish council of religious leaders, who would have kicked him out of the synagogue, Peter boldly responded, "We will not stop obeying God to obey you" (Acts 4:1-22).

It is my deep hope that our journey together has opened up the realm of possibilities to you, that it actually *could be God* who is encouraging you to make the leap out of the fading Church Season and into the emerging

Kingdom Age as you begin to practice the Kingdom principles Jesus is inviting us to live.

The leap can feel like Indiana Jones, as he was teetering on a high ledge above a canyon. He was invited to leap, but all he could see was the unknown danger below. If he wasn't caught, he would become a dead heap on the canyon floor. But, as he took a brave step out, the bridge appeared underneath him, and he was able to walk to the other side.

Do you trust Jesus to catch you and build your bridge to follow Him to the other side?

What will you decide?

REFLECT

- What is your heart saying to you right now?

- If you remove all the "what ifs" in your life, what do you truly long to do?

DO SOMETHING

- Reclaim your Kingdom compass and go where it points you.

EPILOGUE

Imagine being on top of a high mountain where you can see the landscape in the valley below. You see much darkness but spread throughout are twinkling lights. Some are bigger than others. Some are brighter than others, but they all shine into the darkness.

As you look closer, you see the shining lights are groups of people gathered. They are meeting in homes and public spaces, and they are communing with the King. They are all around tables, eating meals, joyfully sharing their lives, everyone gathered belongs. It seems no one person does all the talking, but each person has something valuable to say, and they are listened to and understood.

Sometimes they go outside, and then their lights shine brighter and brighter. The darkness becomes lighter as they follow Jesus' direction to proclaim the Kingdom, cast out demons, cure diseases, and heal the sick. Miracles of healing and heavenly provision follow.

As you continue to observe, you see a collection of lights come together, sharing the unique light their community carries. You see the homeless become housed and the poor becoming prosperous. You see different ethnicities gathering and immigrants enfolded. You see justice and mercy released through the shining lights.

A big screen comes across the sky. You see seven mountains on the screen, and you realize they represent the seven mountains of culture.

The tops of the mountains are very dark, but scattered throughout the mountains, small lights twinkle. Your eyes are opened to see a heavenly battle between the angels of light and the angels of darkness. Suddenly, a streak of light comes across the sky, and you see Jesus the King standing at the top of each mountain. He is beckoning the lights to begin the journey up the mountains.

Some go, but others stay frozen in place. Some leave the mountain all together. But, as you look up, you see thrones being put in place on each mountain. King Jesus takes His place, and you see the thrones are meant for two. The lights that were beckoned to come up the mountain continue their climb. Heavenly angels accompany them. Battles rage, but they continue their journey. They look into King Jesus' face, and it gives them courage to continue the climb.

They reach the top. The angels blow their trumpets and begin to sing. King Jesus walks towards the lights and puts a crown upon their head and a scepter into their hands. He takes their arm and leads them to a table laden with every kind of delicious food and wine ever created. They sit and eat their fill, joyfully sharing and laughing. When the heavenly meal is finished, King Jesus gets up and pulls out their chair as they walk arm in arm down the red carpet towards the throne.

When they sit together on the throne, you discover the whole mountain becomes lit up with brilliant light. It shines out onto the rest of the earth, bringing light and hope to the dark places.

Suddenly, you are given a mirror. You look upon it and see, with surprise, the one who ate with King Jesus at the banqueting table is...*you*. You gasp with delight as you realize you are the one wearing the crown and sitting upon the throne, and because of your willingness to climb the mountain to join King Jesus at His table and on His throne, the mountain went from darkness to brilliant light, giving opportunity for many others to journey within the brilliant light to experience the glory of your King.

MEET TAMARA

Tamara J. Buchan is the Founder and Director of Reclaim Initiative. Tamara completed seminary and was ordained in the Evangelical Covenant denomination. She experienced years of fruitful and fulfilling ministry experience when her path took a very unexpected turn, leading her to break down her boxes around God and her life of faith. Her life has never been the same!

Tamara birthed Reclaim Initiative in 2013 to support, equip, and resource the Body of Christ to reclaim their identities, lives, and generational destinies. Her passion is helping people discover the treasures hidden within them, as they walk together in Kingdom community. She has written nine insightful books on identity and the Kingdom, which are available on www.ReclaimInitiative.com.

Tamara and her husband, Bill, live in beautiful Morrison, Colorado with their two puppies. They have three daughters, two sons-in-law, and two young grandchildren, who keep them very blessed and busy!

"YOU WERE MEANT FOR MORE" SERIES

GREEN EMBRACES: IDENTITY RECLAIMED

A strong handshake, a tender hug, a long embrace...being held feels good. As human beings built for connection, embraces carry power when they come from someone who knows us fully and loves us anyways. The embrace of God's powerfully loving arms began in a green garden long ago. The original design was a clean, lively, and green creation to host and hold people as they were meant to be. To live loved was the original design. We've wandered and gotten lost, lived for less, and walked a winding road. However, the fresh, pure, living embrace of God who knows us as Beloved Child, is available to each of us, right now. It's up to us to reclaim what was ours all along.

Discover that we are truly loved, that our story is part of a greater divine story, that we are forgiven and truly accepted and that we have a true place of belonging. If embraced, these words have the power to bring true freedom, the kind of freedom that can only come when we see ourselves the way that God sees us, a beloved child of the King!

Available in paperback book and eBook

"You Were meant for More" SERIES

SPUN OUT ON SHAME? RECLAIM YOUR SANITY

Shame literally spins us around as isolation, hopelessness, and self-condemnation, become our constant companions. God breaks into the cycle, taking our shame and spinning it into his forgiveness. As we are cleansed and set free, our lives become fresh and fully alive. Spun out on shame? Reclaim Your Sanity, will take you through a journey of exchanging shame for freedom...the life you were meant to experience... You Were meant for More!

Just as washed clothes are hung out to dry in the fresh air, likewise, God wants us to experience a fresh start by going through His "wash cycle," spun out to dry, and then hung in the fresh air. As He washes us with water of His Word, dirty shame is removed for a clean, fresh start... living an abundant life He always meant for us to live!

Available in paperback book and eBook

"YOU WERE MEANT FOR MORE" SERIES

OUR DAD IS NOT MAD: TRUST RECLAIMED

We look out into all the world and see suffering all around us. We wonder what kind of a dad would allow his child to experience a world like this, one full of pain and torment. It's pretty simple to assume that our Dad is Mad.

Perhaps the suffering isn't only out there, but on the inside. Perhaps it was your earthly dad as he betrayed your trust, crushed your spirit, or abused your body. In your child-like state, you couldn't help but make the connection that your heavenly dad is just like your earthly dad, he's mad.

Maybe you were lucky and had an amazing dad. But, life happened, and as one challenging experience after another hit you, the thought began to emerge more often that you must have done something wrong and your dad must be...mad.

Believing our heavenly dad is not mad, but is good and trustworthy is one of the greatest challenges of life. Journey through Our Dad is Not Mad: Trust Reclaimed and discover a trustworthy father who loves you beyond what you could ever imagine.

Available in paperback book and eBook

"YOU WERE MEANT FOR MORE" SERIES

5-STAGES OF IDENTITY: SUCCESS RECLAIMED

Success. The world tells us to believe that success is defined by what we do or by the things we own, but Jesus came to show us a different way to live success. He flipped the order. He taught us to know first WHO we are, and to let our True Identity define our success. Think about it. When Jesus died, he didn't have a job, he didn't own a home, or even a car. He alienated most of the important people around him, two of his friends betrayed him—and most of his other disciples quickly disappeared when he was arrested. Despite it all, if you look for a "Top 10 Most Successful People" in history, you will ALWAYS find Jesus on the list. Why? Jesus understood that success came through living in relationship, first with his loving father, and then with the people around him. He knew the way to the top was to serve and even to sacrifice his life for his friends.

5 Stages of Identity: Success Reclaimed redefines success through the exploration of Jesus' every day life. Jesus modeled valuable lessons for us in each stage of identity. His actions help us identify the pitfalls, give us strategies for the challenges, and provide us with tips for how to navigate the route through earthly success and failure. When we apply Jesus' practical lessons to our lives, we discover ourselves reaching for a success, which ultimately satisfies the longings of our hearts.

Are you ready? Put on your workout clothes so you can exercise reclaimed success at every stage in your identity journey, enabling you to leave your significant imprint upon the world!

Coming soon to Paperback and eBook

IDENTITY CRISIS: RECLAIM THE TRUE YOU

What does a dried dandelion have to do with an identity crisis? Everything, if we stop looking at it from a gardener's perspective and start to understand its hidden value. The identities we adopt from the world are like dandelions the gardener fervently attacks before they dry up into the perfect ball of seeds, which spread all over the yard when the wind begins to blow. If we think about our enemy, the Devil, as the gardener, we begin to understand his motive is to convince us that our identities are worthless weeds: throwaways when compared to the beautiful rose bushes right next to us. Our enemy, the gardener, thrives when we agree that our identities are discarded weeds, rather than boldly reclaiming our true identities from our Master Gardener: the Creator of the Universe. To reclaim is to take that which is worthless and make it beautiful and productive again. An overgrown garden with dried dandelions can appear to be worthless. However, when the Master Gardener begins to blow the seeds, our lives suddenly "wake up" and start to take root in gardens we never dreamed we could inhabit.

Available in Paperback and eBook

IDENTITY CRISIS: RECLAIM THE TRUE YOU COMPANION BIBLE STUDY: PART ONE AND PART TWO

Identity Crisis: Reclaim the True You Study Guide is a 6-week daily process designed to support you as you journey towards reclaiming your Identity, Life and Destiny because you truly were "Meant for More!"

It takes 90 days to build a new brain path, so *Identity Crisis: Reclaim the True You Study Guide* builds on the process of creating new dreams that replace the worn out defeated thoughts that often keep us paralyzed. Partner together with God to discover just how much He is intent on Reclaiming your Identity, Life and Destiny because He knows "You are Meant for More!"

Available in Paperback and eBook

SEEKING THE CHRISTMAS LAMB:
A FAMILY ADVENT HANDBOOK
BOOK 1

Is your Christmas more "Santa" than "Savior"?
Are your Christmas memories more painful than peaceful?
Is your holiday season happy or harried?

The truth is...Christmas isn't what it used to be.

Reclaim Christmas this year with Seeing the Christmas Lamb: A Family
Advent Handbook. Experience new and profound joy joined by deep
and satisfying peace as you discover (again) the treasures of Christmas
long forgotten. Watch as each memorable moment lays a foundational
layer of faith in the hearts and minds of your loved ones—a life-
changing gift to establish a generational legacy. Marvel as the bonds of
rich and lasting connectedness are birthed, sharing the rich tradition of
Advent and anticipating the birth of the One who came to save us.

Reclaim your Christmas. Put your focus back on Christ, the greatest
Christmas gift of all!

Available in hardcover and e-book

COMING SOON:
RECLAIM YOUR GENERATIONAL LEGACY

God gives us an invitation in Jeremiah 33:3, "Call to Me and I will answer you and tell you great and unsearchable things you do not know" (NIV). This is the season God wants to reveal the secret blocks of our past, as well as its treasures. Each family passes on a legacy to the next generation. God intends it to be one of blessing, but, sadly, most often the blessing is lost. It's as if it was buried treasure in the bottom of the sea.

Instead, we've often passed down the destructive sins and curses to our children and to those who follow them. We've done it unknowingly, but God is looking for those who will partner with Him to reclaim their generational legacy, so His blessings can flow and have an impact for a thousand years of blessings!

Now is the season for us to find our hidden or buried blessings, to open up the treasure box and discover the "secret things" that have been unclaimed, sometimes for centuries.

CONNECT WITH US

Now that you've finished Unboxing God: Reclaiming Faith in a Post-Church Culture, some of you may be wondering, where do I go from here?

The transition from the Church Season to the Kingdom Age will be one of the biggest reorientations of your life. Don't do it alone! I'd love to support you in your journey. Reclaim Initiative has a variety of opportunities for continued to support as you take steps to follow Jesus' invitation to "seek first His Kingdom!"

Go to Contact Tamara at ReclaimInitiative.com to receive Unboxing God updates or to schedule a free one on one 20 minute conversation so we can meet one another and discern what will best support you in your Kingdom journey!

Check out the Reclamation Journey:
www.reclaiminitiative.com/reclamation-journey

Follow My blog:
www.reclaiminitiative.com/blog/

Like Reclaim Initiative's Facebook page:
www.facebook.com/ReclaimInitative/

Together with you,
Tamara